HONEYMOONS

CAN KILL

Bob Doerr

Jim West mystery/thriller™

TotalRecall Publications, Inc.
1103 Middlecreek
Friendswood, Texas 77546
281-992-3131   281-482-5390 Fax
www.mousegate.com

Printed in the United States of America with simultaneous printings in Australia, Canada, and United Kingdom.

FIRST EDITION
1 2 3 4 5 6 7 8 9 10

TO LEIGH

AND THE HONEYMOON WE BOTH SURVIVED.

Award Winning Author: Bob Doerr

Award winning author Bob Doerr grew up in a military family, graduated from the Air Force Academy, and had a career of his own in the Air Force. Bob specialized in criminal investigations and counterintelligence gaining significant insight to the worlds of crime, espionage, and terrorism. His work brought him into close coordination with the security agencies of many countries and filled his mind with the fascinating plots and characters found in his books today. His education credits include a Masters in International Relations from Creighton University. A full time author with fifteen published books, Bob was selected by the Military Writers Society of America as its Author of the Year for 2013. The Eric Hoffer Awards awarded *No One Else to Kill* its 2013 first runner up to the grand prize for commercial fiction. Two of his other books were finalists for the Eric Hoffer Award in earlier contests. *Loose Ends Kill* won the 2011 Silver medal for Fiction/mystery by the Military Writers Society of America. *Another Colorado Kill* received the same Silver medal in 2012 and the Silver medal for general fiction at the Branson Stars and Flags national book contest in 2012. In addition to *Honeymoons Can Kill*, Bob has written seven prior novels in the Jim West series. Bob lives in Garden Ridge, Texas, with Leigh, his wife of 46 years, and Cinco, their ornery cat.

The Book

Honeymoons Can Kill is a 68,000 word mystery thriller that is set on a cruise ship in the Gulf of Mexico. The eighth book in the Jim West series, this is the first book to bring back prior characters from previous books. Deputy Rose Luna (*Greed Can Kill*) joins Jim on a five-day cruise out of Galveston, TX, and on the second day of the cruise, the couple encounters Sarah Stone (*Dead Men Can Kill*). Sarah Stone is now Sarah Lassiter having gotten married on the ship right before it left port. When Sarah's new husband is murdered on the second night of the cruise, the cruise changes from a relaxing vacation to a race to catch the killer before everyone disembarks in three more days. The book should be considered as rated PG-13.

Chapter 1

Ed Anderson sat on a bar stool at the counter of the High Seas bar and watched two giggly, young women approach the counter next to him. Both wore very short, cutoff jeans and bikini tops that provided scant protection from an early cold front that seemed determined to ruin this first day of the cruise. They were loud and laughing with a vocabulary that didn't go much past the word "awesome" or the phrase "no way". He watched them in the mirror behind the bar as they left carrying their fancy drinks. Oh, to be young again.

Forcing his mind back to the reason he had chosen this cruise, Ed took another sip of his Coors Light and worked through his plan for the thousandth time. He had never killed anyone before. He had never wanted to, but they had driven him to this point.

After thirty some years of loyal service for Hudson Financial Data Management, they patted him on his back, gave him what even he believed to be a good severance check, and kicked him out the door. Only later did he realize why they let him go, and how the IRS and the state of New York would demand nearly half of his severance check. Even the letter of recommendation they finally wrote for him made him look like a mediocre employee. They had screwed him, and now he would get his revenge.

Always a methodical person, Ed had set about researching the best ways to get away with murder, and the amount of detail and advice he found on the internet floored him. He discarded most of the suggested ways to "safely" kill someone that he ran across during his search, but set aside a number of others for further consideration.

He graded the half dozen possible scenarios before he settled on his final choice. He believed if he could keep his wits about him, his plan would be foolproof. Unfortunately, two innocent people would have to die to confuse the investigators, but as he had discovered in his research, misdirection was a key aspect to any good plan.

The internet also provided him with some interesting advice on how to get his weapons through security and onto the ship. Of course, it wasn't as simple as a "how to" manual, but almost. His search of the internet surprised him with how many would-be authors, and as many movie fans, shared and debated ideas on the topic. One, in particular, had proved accurate, as he had been able to smuggle four "nasty" blades aboard in the soles of his boots. The trick he discovered was to ensure the blades fit together in a shape that covered the entire sole of each boot. It took time and some effort to find someone who could make them, but in the end the effort succeeded.

In fact, looking back, he had the most difficulty in determining when and where to take his revenge. When he discovered that Joe Lassiter, the man he wanted dead, had booked reservations on this ship, he saw it as the omen for which he had been waiting. Tonight his first victim would die, and he wondered who it would be.

Chapter 2

I watched her enter the airport terminal from the ramp to the Southwest 737 that brought her to Houston Hobby from El Paso. She saw me and smiled, and I waved back. Despite being well into my forties, divorced, and having known Deputy Rose Luna for a few months, I had to resist the urge to flee.

"Coward," I said to myself but loud enough for a nearby person to turn and look at me. A number of factors played into my irrational desire to escape.

The few friends I have thought my taking a cruise with Rose was great, long overdue, and something that would help me finally get over my divorce. One friend kept saying to me, "Jim West, you lucky guy," and gave me a thumbs up every time he ran into me in the last month or so.

I knew I was lucky, but I also believed I had gotten over my divorce long ago. It hadn't been easy. I never saw the divorce coming, and when my ex walked out on me, it hit me like a truck. Looking back, I realize now that I hadn't been the most attentive husband, and after the divorce, I became "risk adverse" when it came to women. My self-confidence took a hit, but that was more than a few years ago, and time had done its healing.

What bothered me now, or at least what I told myself, was that I wasn't much of a conversationalist or an entertainer. Other than the obvious, what was I supposed to do for the next five days without boring or antagonizing Rose? And yes, I did select the shortest cruise travelling in and out of Galveston.

"Jim," Rose said, as she passed through the security point and approached me.

I smiled, and we kissed.

"How was the flight?" I asked, taking her hand as we walked toward the baggage area.

"Easy and short," she said.

"Your hair has grown out," I said.

"Not really." She pulled back a patch of her straight black hair disclosing a nasty scar. "The magic of a comb over. Never again will I make snide remarks about men trying to hide their bald heads with a comb over."

"Well, your hair looks beautiful, and no one can see the scarring."

"Ha!" she said but kept her smile.

"What's the latest with the job?"

"Nothing's changed since the last time we talked. I think I'm ready to get back to work, but the sheriff thinks I need more time off. He never liked my running off to New Mexico, despite the FBI's request for our support. My guess is he would be happy if I quit."

"No one could blame you if you did," I said.

She gave me a look that said we've been through all this before, and we had, although not in the last month. I stayed away from the topic in our recent phone calls, because I knew it was a touchy subject. I made a quick decision right there to stay away from the topic on the cruise, too.

"Do you think I'm too short?" she asked while we waited for her suitcase to appear on the conveyer belt.

"Not at all. What brought that up?"

"All the young women these days are tall." She nodded her heads toward a nearby pair of tall teenage girls.

"No they aren't, and besides, I think you're the perfect height."

"I'd like to be five six."

"You're close enough."

"I'm a couple inches short. There it is," she said, pointing to her blue travel bag.

I grabbed her single suitcase, and we left the airport. The drive to the port in Galveston didn't take long. Our conversation during the drive centered on the flooding in this part of Texas from the hurricane the year before. Signs of the damage could still be seen. Neither one of us talked about the upcoming cruise except to say a few times that it should be fun.

After arriving at the cruise terminal, we checked our luggage and joined the long security line to board the ship in plenty of time to make the cruise.

"Hey, this is crazy," she said looking around the large terminal. "Are all these people going on our cruise?"

"I think so. If we had a lot of cruises under our belts, we could head over to that line," I pointed to the other side of the large room.

"That doesn't look short either."

"I think in this case, short is relative," I said.

"I can't believe we're really doing this," Rose said.

"Why?"

She laughed. "It's not just me, you're more nervous than a teenager on his first date."

"No way."

"Don't get me wrong, I'd much rather have you this way. I'd hate it if I sensed all you had on your mind was getting me alone in the cabin. But, I was worried you might cancel at the last moment."

"Rose, the thought never entered my mind."

She stared at me, and I finally had to grin. She hit me on the arm and smiled back.

"I wouldn't have blamed you. Why should you keep a pity based promise made to a scar faced woman in a coma?"

"Come on, you're a beautiful woman, so quit saying those things about yourself. Besides, why do you think I'm not waiting to get you alone? You won't have a gun this time."

"I could take you without a gun." Despite the tough talk, she reached around my arm and clasped it against her.

Deputy Sheriff Rose Luna had gotten involved in a mess I had created a few months earlier. The mess involved a missing briefcase, a Mexican cartel, the FBI, and even a ghost town. In the process, she had been shot in the head and almost died. Before that happened, and at no particular moment I could remember, I had fallen for her. And yes, while she was in a coma near death at a hospital in Las Cruces, New Mexico, I promised, among other things, to take her on a cruise if she would wake up. Somehow, she heard me and remembered my promise. That she heard me was a surprise. That she held me to the promise surprised me more.

We weaved back and forth between the ropes that helped keep discipline in the line and followed a couple from Oklahoma who seemed to have no ability to be quiet and not bother us. Well, it bothered me, but Rose appeared to enjoy talking to them.

The conversation met all the typical topics for a conversation between strangers in a line waiting to get on a cruise ship. Have you cruised much, been on this ship before, where are you from, are you taking any excursions, etc., etc.? Rose handled most of our responses, as did the other woman. The other guy and I kept most of our involvement in the conversation to a few grunts and head nods. At one point, he asked me if I watched the game last night. I didn't know to which game he referred, but I told him I had been traveling.

When we finally arrived at the front of the line, we went to different spots along the processing counter and lost track of them.

"She was nice. They're from Oklahoma, and this is their thirtieth wedding anniversary. I think that's sweet. What did you two talk about?"

"Oh, not much, you know, the game," I said.

The woman behind the counter took all our paperwork and wandered off somewhere.

"Did you get his name?" she asked.

"No."

"Her name is Milly, and she made a point at saying not "Miley". I guess Miley Cyrus is not someone she wants to be lumped with. I thought that was kind of silly, because nothing about her reminds me of Miley."

"You're right about that."

"Did you see the bridal party?"

"What?"

"You weren't listening to us, were you?" she asked.

"No, you were having a nice chat, and I didn't want to interfere. Like I said, we were talking about the game."

"What game?" She had me there.

"Well, we didn't talk much about it."

After we received our boarding documents, we left the hoard of people in the terminal and followed another long line of people heading for the ship. At least this line kept moving at a steady walking pace.

"I like this," Rose remarked when we finally made it to the main lobby of the ship.

A live band played Caribbean music, cruise ship wait staff walked around handing out fancy cocktails, and everyone appeared to be smiling and laughing.

"Where do we get our luggage?" Rose asked.

"They'll bring it to our room."

"That's right, I remember now. Want to go to our cabin and drop off this stuff?" she held up her carryon and purse. I nodded, and we left the lobby.

The cabin we selected came with a balcony. Situated on the eighth deck and mid-ship, we hoped the effects of any rough seas would be less there than elsewhere on the ship. Rose had never been on a cruise and worried about how well she could handle the seas.

"It's a bit chilly now, but the weather for the rest of the cruise is supposed to be good," I said. "Tomorrow, while we are at sea, we should be able to sit out here on the balcony and enjoy the view."

"Will we be able to see any whales?"

"No, I don't think so. We might see dolphins and flying fish, but whales don't migrate through here."

"Flying fish aren't real, are they?"

"I'll show you some. I'm pretty sure we'll see some."

"I'll settle for dolphins. When do you think our luggage will arrive?" Rose asked.

"I've only been on a handful of cruises, but I think it takes a couple hours. They'll leave it outside the door. Would you like to explore the ship or get a drink somewhere?"

"Maybe later, but right now I think we should check out the bed." She pulled me from the balcony and onto the bed.

Chapter 3

Ed's first victim needed to be someone who worked for the cruise line, since his plan involved throwing initial suspicion away from the real target and, of course, himself. He believed the ship's leadership would want to keep the incident quiet. Certainly they would believe another crew person did it. After all, why would a guest murder someone he or she didn't know? Then, when a second murder occurred and the victim turned out to be a passenger, what would the police - no they didn't really have police out here - what would the ship's security people think?

A third killing would be optimum for throwing investigators in an all together different direction, but it would also be the most risky. He would have to decide on that later. At the moment, he needed to find a suitable first victim.

The weather with its low clouds, strong breeze and light rain seemed perfect for murder. The sea had become a little rough. Not bad, he thought, but enough to keep most people off the promenade deck.

He selected the time, eleven o'clock at night, based on his research. Two different blog sites contained comments claiming a person could move about in the dark at that time without raising much suspicion, because it wasn't too late. Additionally, the comments claimed the chances of running into other people at that time of night were low. He had walked his neighborhood at eleven at night on three different occasions and believed the comments had merit. He ran into the same dog walker twice and had exchanged greetings about how nice, quiet, and peaceful it was, but observed no one else.

"Much better to get some exercise in now, than when everyone's out in the morning," the woman walking the dog had said.

Well, he didn't expect to run into any dog walkers on the ship. In fact, as he stood there in the pitch black of the rear of the ship, he started to wonder if he would encounter anyone at all. The cool temperature started to get to him despite the hooded sweatshirt he wore. He waited in a spot out of the wind funneling down the sides of the ship, but every now and then, a bit of wind swirled around and reached him.

The noise from the churning water in the wake behind the ship, the wind, and the ship's engines all blended into a steady sound that after twenty minutes seemed to evolve into the silence of white noise, not unlike the sound his daughter played in his grandson's room to help him sleep.

Several hours earlier at this very spot, he had a conversation with a crewman from the Philippines.

"What are you doing?" he had asked.

The crewman, kneeling above a metal plate from which he scraped off the old paint, looked up at him. "Putting new paint on these," he said in accented English and pointed at seven plates next to each other. Each plate looked to be twelve inches square. The other six plates had paint that appeared worn and in need of a new coat. The man had the plate he was working on almost entirely stripped.

"Looks like you would never get done doing all the metal plates on the ship."

Looking up at Ed, the crewman grinned, "We don't. I will work for two more hours and then come back tomorrow. After I leave, another man will come here and work tonight."

The two chatted for a while longer. The crewman seemed to appreciate the break from work. By the time he left, Ed hoped this same worker wouldn't be the one whom he would kill tonight.

Ed's solitude finally ended when a person carrying a bucket and some tools approached his location. He backed deeper into the dark shadows and watched the crewman approach. This person was not the one he had talked to earlier in the day.

It didn't matter if the man saw him or not; he had a right to be there. However, the lone crewman never noticed him. The crewman squatted over the metal plates, and facing the water, he placed the bucket and his tools on the deck next to him. He fastened a small lantern onto one of the guard rails and turned it on.

The dim light surprised the soon-to-be killer. Why hadn't he anticipated a light? It only made sense with the lack of lighting here at the stern of the ship.

Too late to over think this, Ed told himself, and feeling strangely determined, he took four quick steps to reach the man.

Chapter 4

"Are you really going to eat all that bacon?" Rose asked the next morning at breakfast.

"The pieces stuck together. I didn't think it would be okay for me to put food back after it was on my plate."

She continued to stare at my plate.

"Want some?"

She reached over and took a couple of slices. "We may have to skip lunch."

I grinned. "We're on a cruise. We're supposed to overeat and be lazy. Besides you're a lot thinner than you were when I met you."

"I had trouble eating anything at the hospital, and when I went home, I didn't seem to ever have an appetite. I'm actually at the weight I'm supposed to be for my height."

"Well, you're on a cruise now, so eat up. I'm just trying to lead by example."

"By the way," Rose said, looking at two of the ship's officers huddled together in serious conversation not far from our table, "have you paid attention to the ship's crew this morning?"

"Not at all. Why?"

"Something's going on."

"Think we're sinking?" I said and watched the two officers walk away.

"Funny. No, I'm being serious. Something is going on with the crew."

"Well, true story, I was on a cruise one time that ran out of bacon. I doubt if it's any worse than that."

She gave me a frustrated shake of the head. "Okay, be that way, but when the pirates board the ship, don't act surprised."

Rose left the table and returned to the buffet line grabbing a couple of cinnamon rolls for us.

"That's my girl," I said when she plopped one on my plate.

After eating, we decided to walk a lap or two around the ship. We found the promenade on the fifth deck.

"Nice out here," I remarked as we started our walk. The chill from the day before had disappeared, and thanks to a trailing wind, we felt only a slight breeze.

We strolled towards the stern of the ship, stopping on occasion to stare out over the railing at the Gulf. Different shades of blue blended together to form the horizon.

"Doesn't look like a lake, that's for sure," Rose said.

"It must have taken tremendous bravery for the first sailors to leave sight of land and see nothing but ocean around them," I said.

"I couldn't have done it," Rose said.

We continued our walk and discovered yellow tape and a few cones blocking the stretch of the promenade that went around the stern of the ship. At first, I thought the crew must be doing some maintenance or cleaning to this stretch of decking, but then two of the ship's officers walked out of the area.

"What's going on?" Rose asked.

They looked at us and one of them shook his head rather than say anything. As they passed by, I noticed the shorter guy carried a small box containing what I believed to be crime scene gloves.

"I knew something was up," Rose said to me, her face giving

me that "told-you-so" look.

"Think maybe someone fell over?" I asked.

"Wouldn't we be circling around looking for someone if they had?"

"That may have happened while we were still sleeping. And you know, without any landmarks that we can see out there, we wouldn't know if we were going around in a big circle right now," I said. "Well, I guess that's not right, we could tell from the sun."

"I thought the military would have taught you how to navigate."

"I wasn't in the navy."

"So, what do you think happened?" she asked.

"A nasty fight or assault?"

"Maybe someone got killed."

"Don't say that. I'll feel like I jinxed the ship," I said.

"Jim, whatever happened here has nothing to do with you. We don't know anyone on the ship, we don't have any reason to get involved, and no one is going to tell us anything about what happened anyway."

It didn't take long for us to find out how wrong Rose was.

Chapter 5

Rose and I joined a trivia contest in the Lido bar area later in the morning and discovered neither one of us knew much about pop music from the first decade of the twenty first century. In fact, our almost total lack of answers resulted in our not even handing our answers in to be scored.

"Do you feel as old as I do?" Rose asked as we were leaving the bar.

"Not knowing what people twenty years younger than you like in music does not make a person old. If they asked about music in the eighties or nineties, we would have rocked."

"Or Tejano music," she said, grinning.

Although we had only reached the first hour of the lunch period, we did what most of the other people on the cruise did and headed back to the large buffet setup at the front of the ship. When we entered the room, the scene reminded me of fire ants attacking a grasshopper they had captured. Crowds of people were fighting their way into and out of the space around the food. While the ship designers may have envisioned polite lines peacefully going up and down each row or around the circular displays, it appeared only those people with frustrated looks on their faces actually waited in line.

I sympathized with them, but I also knew if later I felt like I needed two more drumsticks or another scoop of cobbler, I would be one of those "in-and-out" raiders. Of course to start with, and because of Rose's presence, we got in line and agreed with those around us mumbling about the creeps taking cuts ahead of us.

It took a while to find an empty table, but we did finally manage to do so. I had barely taken my seat when I heard my name being called.

"Jim! Jim West, is that you?"

I looked up and saw a woman from my past hurrying toward me. She gave me a big hug, and a flood of mixed emotions raced through me. Out of the corner of my eye, I saw Rose studying the situation.

She didn't look the same. Her blond hair had been tinted red and flowed past her shoulders. She also looked older than the handful of years should have caused. I wondered if I did, too.

"Sarah, Sarah Stone, is that you?"

She leaned away a little, but her right hand still clung to my arm. "I'm no longer a Stone, Jim. Now I'm a Lassiter." She held up her hand and showed off a wedding ring along with a diamond that looked too big to be out of a locked safe.

"Well, congratulations –"

"Sarah, what are you doing?"

I looked up and saw a tall, thin man reach out and remove Sarah's hand from my arm.

"I think this couple wants to eat their lunch," he said.

She let the man remove her hand, smiling at him and then back at me. Something in the smile didn't look right.

"Joe, this is Jim West, an old friend. A very important old friend," Sarah said.

"Nice to meet you, Joe" I said and extended my hand. Joe took my hand and squeezed more than necessary. Decked out in white slacks and a light blue button up shirt, he looked like he might be going to a film shoot rather than to lunch on a cruise ship.

"Joe is my husband. We were married yesterday on the ship."

"Oh, that was your wedding?" Rose asked joining in on the conversation.

"There were two weddings, we found out, but it could have been," Sarah said.

"Sarah and Joe, this is my friend, Rose," I said.

While the three exchanged hellos, I immediately regretted referring to Rose as a friend and not something more appropriate. What should I have called her? I didn't know the answer, so I hoped my comment had passed unnoticed.

Rose mentioned something about seeing a bridesmaid in a pink dress, and Sarah acknowledged that her bridesmaids did wear pink dresses.

"If I knew you two were going to be on the ship, I would have invited you, Jim," Sarah said. "We only had a handful of guests."

"Did any of them stay for the cruise?" I asked, knowing that the ceremonies usually occur right before the ship's departure to allow guests who are not travelling time to leave.

"My maid of honor and a few other friends. You'll have to meet them."

"We should all do dinner tonight or tomorrow," Rose said.

"Sounds like a plan," Joe said and tugged at Sarah's arm. "Let's let them eat."

"One second," Sarah said, and I thought I caught a little frustration in her voice. She pulled a small tablet of paper and a pen out of her pants pocket. She wrote on it and tore off the sheet of paper. "Here, Jim, leave a message at our room and give us a time and place to meet you tomorrow night."

"We will," Rose said before I could reply.

The two walked away.

"Someone I should know about?" Rose said grinning.

"It's a long story, but we had an adventure not unlike the one you and I had a few months ago."

"Nothing more? She seemed awful clingy."

"I wondered about that too. For someone who just got married. I got a silly vibe that everything wasn't alright."

"Buyer's remorse?" Rose asked. "You know, sort of like cruise remorse."

"I don't have any remorse," I said before I realized she was teasing me again and was probably talking about herself. "Hope you don't."

"Not unless I find out you have more old girlfriends on the ship."

"She wasn't really a girlfriend."

"Just a friend, like me?"

Ouch.

Chapter 6

Later that afternoon, while Rose and I listened to a piano player in the Aft Bar, Ed Anderson watched a crewman leave the men's restroom by the casino and reopen it for public use. He had watched the same worker clean it the evening before. The restroom could be seen from the casino, but its presence was more obvious to the people leaving the theater.

It would make a good place to kill the pompous Joe Lassiter, Ed thought, not seeing any security cameras near the restroom, but how would he get him into the restroom alone?

Ed moved out to the deck and walked to mid ship before entering near the ship's shopping area. He realized he felt younger today, and he even had a little spring in his step. He believed his murder of the crewman the night before would never be linked to him, and tonight, he had a new, more important target.

Abstract thoughts crossed his mind. Was this how a submarine captain felt as he closed on his target with torpedoes at the ready, or how a bomber pilot felt moments before he released his bombs on target?

Ed had selected four locations on the ship as options to where he would kill Lassiter. He liked the restroom by the casino, but any of them would work. With so many passengers on the ship, he wondered how much he had to do to alter his appearance. Not much, he thought, but still, some disguise would be necessary. Looking at his watch, he realized the time had come to start the pursuit of his prey.

While finding someone on a ship with thousands of passengers might normally be a difficult task, he had done his homework by eavesdropping on a group of women he had seen hanging around with Lassiter. He heard one of the women talking with the others about their having set dinner reservations for the early seating during the cruise. Last night he had no trouble locating them in the dining room. Unless they changed plans, Joe Lassiter and his friends should be eating there again this evening.

Returning to his room, Ed put on a black long sleeve shirt, a pair of workman's khaki pants with large pockets on the legs, and a pair of cloth Croc loafers. He filled his pockets with what he needed and put on a Yankees ball cap before leaving.

Tonight didn't have to be the night; he had three more nights on the ship, but he wanted to get this over. He had considered killing Lassiter while he took an excursion off the ship at one of the stops, but he decided that would be a lot more difficult. No, tonight he would find him, get him alone, and kill him.

Thirty minutes later, he verified Lassiter's presence at a table with his friends in the main dining room. Ed knew they might be a while, so he found a spot to sit and wait. From his position in a common use lounge area, he could see the entrance, or in this case, the exit from the dining room that Lassiter would most likely use. His location also offered a view of the water, but the early evening twilight prevented him from seeing much.

He wondered if Lassiter would even recognize him. Probably not, he thought. Lassiter didn't have much time with the company, but of course, he didn't need much time there. Lassiter had family connections. Besides, he didn't seem the type to care about others. He had never spoken a word to him, never stopped by to wish him luck, and Lassiter had even thrown away the commemorative coin Ed had received from a friend in the 101st Airborne. Ed had inadvertently left the coin behind in a drawer with an assortment of pens and notepads.

Ed had called Agnes, his secretary, when days after being forced out of the company, he realized he had forgotten the coin, only to be told by her that Lassiter had thrown it away the day he moved into the office. Agnes claimed she even tried to get it from Lassiter, but Lassiter insisted that if it was important, it wouldn't have been left behind. She also said the guy didn't like the military. Reason enough to kill him, Ed now thought.

The knowledge that he couldn't overpower Lassiter, or that his intended target had youth on his side, didn't cause Ed to have a moment's hesitation. He had the element of surprise and a foolproof plan. He felt like a lion waiting and watching for his prey to saunter by. Thinking about his past, he decided he should never have settled for a desk job. He would have made one hell of a government assassin.

Smiling at the thought, Ed even knew what he would've called himself: "The Wind".

"Perfect," he whispered. The wind could go anywhere, but one couldn't see it or control it. The wind could sneak by as a soft breeze or blow by like a hurricane, leaving havoc in its wake.

The more he thought about it, the more it made sense. Didn't all the famous mafia hit men have nicknames? Machinegun Kelly, Baby Face Nelson, and then there were the war spies like Mata Hari. Did anyone know her real name? He would have to do some research on secret identities and imagined there would be a lot of information on the topic on the internet. One thing he knew already, he had to keep everything about his being "The Wind" separate from his daily life.

Dozens of passengers walked by the man in a dark shirt sitting alone on the chair, and while more than half glanced at the man, none made any note of him, and none had the slightest idea that he intended to kill another person that night.

Ed, who now thought of himself as The Wind, focused on the variety of possibilities that could occur over the next few hours. He had to be flexible and realized that despite having selected good locations for the murder, he had to seize the opportunity when and where it came. In the end, there were only a couple rules: no witnesses and an escape path.

After waiting for nearly an hour, he observed Lassiter along with five other men and women emerge from the dining room. Most carried glasses of wine in their hands. The group stopped in the lounge and debated what to do next.

"I don't want to go see any ice skaters," Lassiter said. His voice sounded a little more combative than it needed to be.

"Come on, Joe, you promised," a woman in the group said.

Ed sat in silence, pretending to study a brochure he had picked up earlier, but really listening to the conversation. He wondered if the pretty woman who had admonished Lassiter was his new wife. Someone should have warned her that her new husband was a prick.

"He doesn't have to go if he doesn't want to. He'll just spoil the fun for the rest of us, if he does." This time the voice came from a man who looked a little older than the rest of the group.

The group's conversation turned to things to do in Cozumel once they arrived. Most of the group had signed up for an excursion, and those on the excursion tried to convince the others to join them. Finally, all but Lassiter and the woman walked off.

"You sure you don't mind if I go to the show with them?" the woman Ed imagined to be Lassiter's wife asked.

"I don't care what you do," Lassiter growled.

"Oh, come on, Joe."

"I'm going out for a breath of fresh air," he said and walked away from her. She hastened after him and locked her arm in his.

Ed stood and followed, but he stayed a good distance away from the couple. "I'm The Wind," he said softly and let his new imaginary persona, The Wind, take charge. Role playing, he thought, and it surprised him how calm he became. He watched as the couple went out into the darkness of the deck. He paused long enough not to look like he chased after them before he followed the two, keeping his head down. He stopped inside the exit at a spot where he could see them together outside on the deck. He thought the ship might have numerous security cameras, and later, security personnel would scrutinize this area looking at whatever digital video coverage they could find.

"What should I do?" Ed silently asked his new persona.

"Patience," The Wind answered. "I will tell you when."

He waited for three minutes before he saw the woman return through the same doorway she and her husband had used a few moments earlier.

"Now," The Wind whispered inside Ed's mind.

He casually walked to the doors and out into the night. The sudden blast of wind almost took his hat off. He grabbed it and held it on. Once away from the doorway the air became calmer, but a good breeze still ran down the side of the ship. The smell of the salt air seemed stronger, and the sound of the ship moving through the water reminded him of the night before. A partial moon floated low in the horizon and gave off scant light. A grin formed on Ed's face.

"Walk to the rail and look out at the sea," The Wind whispered inside his mind, and he did. "You're just like any other passenger. Now look around and find your prey."

He saw Lassiter leaning against the rail a little farther towards the stern of the ship. As he watched, Lassiter began walking away from him.

"That's good. Look how it gets darker down there. One of the outdoor lights must be out. Hurry now," The Wind silently instructed.

Ed heeded the voice in his head and walked after Lassiter. Glancing around, he saw no one else out on the deck. Lassiter paused and leaned against the railing, looking out at the ocean.

"Joe? Joe Lassiter is that you?"

Lassiter looked at the man approaching him. "Yes, do I know you?"

"We've met, but you probably don't remember me. So what brings you out here in the dark?" The Wind had total control now.

Lassiter looked at the man with mixed emotions of curiosity and frustration for being bothered. "I'm just getting a breath of fresh air before heading to the theater to join my wife. Excuse me for asking, but what's your name?" Lassiter moved away from the rail.

Ed moved with him stepping in a little closer, making Lassiter feel uncomfortable and back deeper into the shadows.

"I'm sorry, I should've given you my name," he paused for effect. "God! What is that, a dead cat?" he pointed at what looked like a towel on the deck next to the wall.

"What? No that's only a towel," Lassiter said.

"Next to it, look closer."

Lassiter did the expected. He hunched over far enough for The Wind to swing the sharp blade and slam it into the spot in the back of Lassiter's neck where the spine meets the brain stem. Death came at once, while amazingly little blood shot out at impact.

Ed stayed long enough to confirm Lassiter would never be a witness against him and to move the body closer to the wall. The body would be discovered in the morning, but someone strolling by tonight in the darkness shouldn't notice it. While still in the shadows, he flung the steel blade and Lassiter's wallet out into the water below.

Ed walked toward the front of the ship until he reached the last door that led into the ship's interior. He felt strange, like he somehow had relegated control of himself to this other persona, his imaginary alter ego, The Wind. Although less notable, he remembered he had had a similar feeling the night before, when he had killed the crewman. He didn't dwell on the feeling long.

Ed left the promenade, entering the area between the casino and the theater and encountered dozens of people mingling in the corridor. He had to walk through the cluster of people outside the restroom. The crowd had a soothing effect on Ed. He entered the restroom and went immediately to an empty stall. He needed to change his appearance, but for a full minute, he sat fully clothed on the toilet and relaxed.

Ed removed a folded, large gift bag from one of the large pockets in his slacks and hung it on the hook on the stall's door. Next he pulled out a pair of white shorts, a light blue tee shirt, and flip flops from other pockets. He changed clothes and put the ones he had been wearing including the hat and the eyeglasses into the gift bag. Finally, before leaving the stall, he carefully put on the false moustache.

He walked out of the stall into the crowded restroom.

"Next time buddy, change in your cabin! We've been waiting a while out here," a man growled.

"Sorry," he mumbled, almost replying that there were two other stalls. He kept his head down.

Out in the corridor, the crowd still mingled. He thought a show had just gotten out, but then he remembered that Lassiter said he was going to the show. This must be the audience waiting to go in. He took his time moving through the crowd to the opposite side of the ship before finding the nearest elevator. He rode the elevator up to the Sky Lounge, where he took a second in the restroom to double check his moustache and overall appearance before grabbing the same bar stool he had sat in the night before. He placed the bag on the floor next to him.

"Hey, Billy, I see the game is starting." Ed noted that the game was halfway through the first quarter but hoped if confronted later, Billy might remember the statement and agree he arrived in the bar earlier than he had.

The Malaysian bartender smiled at him. "A dirty martini again tonight?"

"You have an excellent memory. Yes, please. Where is everyone this evening? Your bar is nearly empty."

"Too early, did you have a good day today?" Billy asked.

"Yes, we did," Ed answered.

Neither Billy nor the man speaking gave a second thought to the word "we".

Chapter 7

Rose and I sipped wine in the After Dark lounge, one of nine bars on the ship, and were about to leave for the late performance in the theater when Sarah and a gaggle of her friends entered the lounge. She looked around and although there were only three couples in the entire bar, she didn't notice me. I didn't know the names of her friends at that moment, but as she introduced them to me moments later, I've included their names in the conversation that took place while the group stood there next to us.

"I could kill him," Sarah said to the group. "He promised to join us at the theater or meet us here afterwards."

"Oh come on, Sarah," Jill said. "You shouldn't say that."

"Oh, I don't know," Matt said. "Men do die on honeymoons. Did you read about the old farmer and his young bride?"

"Don't go there, this is no time for one of your dirty jokes," Sheila said.

"Come on," Matt said still grinning. "Honeymoons can kill ya. We all know that Sarah is too much woman for Joe."

"Matt!" Sarah said. She shook her head like she might at a naughty child. Surrounded by close friends, their support did comfort her, and at the moment, she didn't feel much like defending her husband.

"Well, he missed a good show, and we had a good time without him," Sheila said.

"That's right," Dylan said, "and Matt may not be too far off.

Joe could be in bed sleeping."

"I hope so," Sarah said. "Otherwise…" she left the end of her threat to everyone's imagination.

"Say, isn't that your friend over there," Jill said, pointing towards me.

I waved at her.

"Oh, my, I was so concentrated on locating my missing husband, I didn't even notice you," Sarah said, walking over to our booth. Her friends followed her.

"That's okay," I said. "How has your day gone?"

Rose stood up, and I took the hint.

"Good, except Joe's been a grouch and didn't go to the ice skating show with us."

"How was it? Jim and I are heading there in a few minutes for the late show," Rose said.

"It was good," Sarah said.

"It was fantastic," Sheila said.

Dylan, standing close behind her, rolled his eyes and grinned.

"Jim, these are my best friends. This is Sheila and her husband Dylan. As you can tell, he robbed the cradle."

They both smiled. Dylan gave Sheila a quick squeeze, and stuck out his hand. While we shook hands, Sarah continued with the introductions.

"And this is Jill my number one, favorite cousin."

"Hi, Jim, and you're Rose, right?" Jill said and extended her hand to Rose.

"Yes, nice to meet you."

"Sorry," Jill said. "Sometimes Sarah can only think of the men in her life."

"Okay, okay, I didn't mean to ignore you, Rose," Sarah said.

"That's alright," Rose said.

"And finally, Matt, meet Jim and Rose," Sarah said.

Matt, standing a little further back and off to the side, smiled and nodded.

"Part of the wedding party?" Rose asked.

"Yes," Sheila answered. "Most of the group couldn't stay for the cruise."

"Well, I'm glad you all did," Sarah said.

"No way was I going to miss it," Jill said. "Say, Jim, Rose, the ice show is going to be performed again in two days on the cruise, why don't you both stay here and have a few drinks with us? For years, I've wanted to meet you."

The you she referred to was me. I started to beg off, not really wanting to get into a discussion about my few days long ago with Sarah. Rose, however, couldn't have been more delighted.

"Are you sure we won't be in the way?" Rose asked.

"Please stay," Sarah said. "If you don't, Jill will be pestering me all night."

"Is this the guy that rescued you and that girl back in New Mexico?" Matt asked.

"The one and only," Sarah said.

"You'll have to tell me about it," Rose said.

The women seemed to take that as a signal, and all started walking to a nearby table, leaving Matt, Dylan and me to grab chairs at an adjacent table.

"So Jim, or is it James?" Dylan asked. Upon closer scrutiny, he didn't seem much older than the others. He kept his dark brown hair short, which might have enhanced a more mature look.

"Always been a Jim," I said.

"So what do you do? Are you like a private eye?"

"No, Dylan, never been a private eye or anything like it. I just seem to stumble into things. At least I should be safe out here on a cruise."

"Oh, I don't know, Sarah is already talking about killing Joe, if he doesn't straighten up. It may just be the newlywed jitters, but something's going on," Dylan said.

"Admit it," Matt said, "none of us think he was a great choice." Matt's light brown hair was shaggy. I couldn't tell if it needed to be combed, or if he never combed it. His face appeared to be a little puffy, and he wore a gold chain around his neck. He spoke with a strong New York accent, stronger than anyone else in the group, which made me wonder if he was the only native New Yorker in the group.

"Let's don't go there," Dylan said. "As you can see, Jim, we're part of the bride's contingent."

"Is there a contingent here with the groom?"

"No, his parents, sister, and a couple of friends who attended the ceremony all left afterwards. They aren't the most sociable family around," Matt said.

"Sort of like the stereotype for the snooty rich," Dylan added.

"And Joe fits that mold perfectly," Matt said.

I noticed both Matt and Dylan wore expensive watches and nicer shirts than what I brought with me, and I couldn't help but wonder if they weren't wealthy, too. Looking over at the women, I saw that all of them seemed to be better attired than either Rose or me, not that my shorts and ten year old Hawaiian shirt weren't cool.

"I imagine things will work themselves out between the two," I said. "He may have just wanted to be alone for a while."

"I thought he might be in the casino," Dylan said. "So while the girls hit the restroom after the show, Matt and I looked around in there, but we didn't see him."

"He said he would meet you here?"

"Yes," they both answered in unison.

"He'll probably show up," I said.

"I think so, too," Matt said. "So, was it you that killed that guy in New Mexico?"

That question caught me off guard, and Dylan caught my reaction.

"Matt, come on."

"No, we were all there, but a cop took out the serial killer, not me."

"Sarah sure implied you rescued her from him," Matt said.

"I may have played a role in it, but it was a long time ago, and incidents like that I try to keep out of my mind," I said.

Matt ignored my attempt at ending the discussion. "You know she wrote an article about it. We've all read it. You've read it, too, haven't you?"

"Yes, of course, but for me spending too much time thinking about it only makes sleeping that much harder."

"Oh," Matt said finally catching on. "Sorry, Sarah doesn't like to talk about it either any more. Guess it's like PTSD or something."

"So where do you live now?" Dylan asked changing the subject.

We continued with our small talk for another thirty minutes. Rose finally rescued me, standing and telling everyone that she had promised me an ice cream sundae earlier in the day and thought she had better fulfill her promise.

"Sorry about that," I said once we were alone in the elevator.

"Don't be. That was great. I understand you wrote love letters to Sarah after she left New Mexico." The smirk on her face told me that it was going to be a long night.

"That's not fair," I said. "Did Sarah tell you?"

"No, she was the perfect former lover."

I tried to interrupt, but Rose put a finger to my lips. At least one of us was having a great time.

"It was her cousin who mentioned the letters. Actually, I think her cousin is the one with the crush on you. I can see a little something in Sarah's eyes, too, when she talks about you, but I think it's Jill I better watch out for. For a cousin, she has a darker complexion than Sarah. I think she's pretty, but I also think she may have been enhanced a little."

"Isn't she with Matt?" I asked, smiling at her reference to Jill's breasts.

"I guess so, but we didn't talk about anyone but you. I'm going to have to find the article Sarah wrote about that incident, since you don't talk about it."

"You didn't even discuss the missing husband?" I asked in another attempt to get the topic away from me.

"Now that is an interesting matter. They've only been married a little over a day, and I sensed a lot of anxiety." Rose paused for a moment. "That may not be the right word, but at least there seemed to be a lack of enthusiasm over the whole marriage thing."

"That's too bad."

"Well, all us women know that you men are creeps, so it shouldn't surprise us." Her tone came out a little harsher than expected, by either of us.

"Have I already messed up?" I asked.

"No, I'm sorry, you've been sweet, and I have no regrets about being here with you," she said and then added, "so far."

"Then what's there to be sorry about?"

"Joe's apparently been a jerk since the wedding. It just made me think of a few men I have known." She shook her head, before smiling and reaching out to hold my hand. "Don't ever be a jerk."

"I wouldn't even know how."

"Well, she tried to play it down, but Sarah is furious at him for standing her up."

"Why would a guy do that?"

"You're the guy, tell me."

"I have no idea. I wouldn't be standing her up."

My comment resulted in a quick elbow to my ribs.

"Ouch!"

"Jerk!" she said but wrapped her arm around mine and squeezed.

"Let's talk about something else. They need to solve their own problems, and I don't think we need to contact them tomorrow about getting together. We may not see them again on the cruise," I said.

We joined the crowd in the casino, where I watched Rose slowly lose twenty dollars at the penny slots. I glanced around but never saw Joe Lassiter.

Chapter 8

I woke up the next morning a few minutes after seven. Rose showed no signs of waking up, so I dressed making as little noise as possible. After leaving a note on the bathroom sink, I left in search of coffee.

Despite the early hour, the moving masses of people that I saw yesterday had already started to build throughout the ship. I found one of the smaller "feeding stations" that had trays of pastries set up and a few urns of coffee. I grabbed a cup of coffee and a couple small cinnamon rolls before moving to a small table with a view out to the water.

I could see land not too far off to the southeast. Our first stop, Cozumel, should be out there somewhere. We hadn't signed up for an excursion and planned to walk around the city for a couple of hours. I felt relaxed and carefree until three officers of the cruise line walked by.

"They're crazy to have us let everyone off the ship like nothing happened!" the man with the most bars on his shoulders said.

"What are we supposed to do? We can't treat a few thousand passengers all as suspects," the man who looked a lot older, but with one less bar on each shoulder, said.

They continued talking but moved past me, and I could no longer hear them. I wondered about the section of the ship Rose and I had encountered cordoned off the day before. My imagination kicked off another scenario in my mind that seemed highly unlikely but motivated me to take my coffee out for an early morning stroll.

Initially, I went out by the large swimming pool and then forward to the hot tubs and up a deck to the jogging track. Nothing looked out of the ordinary. I took the elevators down to the fifth floor and out onto the promenade on the port side. I saw a half dozen or so people leaning against the railings and looking out at the water. I entered the ship and crossed over to the other side and almost walked into the glass doors as they didn't automatically open. I took a step back and looked for a button to push.

"Sir, this side of the ship is closed."

I turned and saw a member of the crew. Like the other ship's officers I saw earlier, she wore a blue uniform. Her uniform sported one gold bar on each shoulder. She stood nearly as tall as me, and her deep blue eyes gave away a degree of nervousness that seemed unwarranted.

"Is everything okay?" I asked, looking at her name tag. Besides learning her name, I saw that she was from Poland.

"Yes."

I thought she wanted to say more but didn't.

"Inga, how long have you been working on this ship?" I asked. The question came out without much thought behind it. I might have asked it in any circumstance. She would easily rate a nine or ten on any man's scale and had likely become tired of men staring at her long before she got out of high school. While I have to admit that I enjoyed standing a few feet from her, I also wanted to know what had the crew so uptight.

"One year," she said.

"How do you like it?"

"It is …." she paused for a second like she needed time to get to the right word. "It is difficult, but I like it."

"Hang in there," I said and started to walk away. I stopped. "Inga, can you really not tell me what is going on out there?"

She studied me for a second. "Not now, but if you give me your name, I will tell you as soon as I can."

I told her my name and cabin number. She smiled when I mentioned my cabin number. I had little doubt that she wanted to be able to identify me to her superiors as someone very interested in whatever it was that she wouldn't tell me, and that her subtle offer to come tell me personally was just a tease to have me identify myself to her.

A decade or so ago, I might have thought that there was something special about me, but unlike some men who never stop believing they're God's gift to women, I've reluctantly become more realistic. I answered her question because it would be suspicious not to, and I had some curiosity about what was going on.

She wrote my information down, nodded at me, and walked over to a nearby chair where she might have been sitting when I tried to use the exit. I hadn't seen her, but I hadn't been looking for anyone either. When she sat down, I returned to the coffee bar, refilled my cup, and made a cup of coffee for Rose.

Rose had gotten up and yelled at me from the bathroom when I entered the room. "I hope you brought me some coffee."

"What if it's not me?"

"If you have coffee, I don't care."

"Funny girl," I said and put the coffee down. "Who would you hope for, if not me?"

"An old man with lots of money."

I laughed, and the door to the bathroom opened.

"It looks like I only got the old man," she said and poked me in the stomach.

"Come on, that's not fair. I've had a hard life."

"I doubt that. What did you do with my coffee?"

I pointed to the small counter. "You know where we were when we ran into the part of the ship that had been cordoned off yesterday morning?"

"Of course."

"Well, they have that entire side of the ship off limits today."

"That makes no sense; it was open all day yesterday. They had only closed off the part at the rear of the boat."

"Today, they have the whole starboard side shut down. And, I heard whom I think might have been the ship's captain talking about how he thought it was a bad idea to let everyone off the ship today like nothing had happened."

"That sounds like trouble. What's going on?"

"I asked Inga that same question. She said she couldn't tell me."

"Who's Inga?"

"Just a crew member guarding the door I was trying to get through," I said.

"Not good. Don't think we're sinking do you?"

"No, that would make no sense."

She grinned. "I think you may be reading too much into this. They may simply be working on the deck or spilled something toxic out there. The remark you overheard may have more to do with trouble in Cozumel than anything on the ship."

"Good point. And here I thought you were just another pretty face."

"Now, Jim, that was a dumb thing to say," she said. I didn't notice any humor in her voice.

"I thought my sense of humor was my best part," I said in hopes of downplaying my remark.

"At times, you can be funny and cute, but comments like that or dumb broad don't add humor to any conversation."

"Point taken," I said, but I wondered about her reaction. I had hit a nerve, a minor nerve, but she definitely didn't like the reference.

"Good. Now the pretty part I like hearing, but not when the implication is that there might not be any brains behind the face." She paused for a second before continuing. "I don't mean to be oversensitive. It's just that for the past four years, I've had the extra duty of bringing a lot of, I guess you could call them, unofficial complaints from the female deputies to the attention of leadership. You know what I mean, nothing specific that would require an investigation, but general behavior that undermines morale and denigrates women."

"Is there a lot of that?"

She gave me a look that implied I was either kidding or stupid. "Too much. The sheriff set up a committee dealing with workplace environment years ago and appointed me to it, along with my role. Supposedly things are supposed to get resolved, but the same issues crop up all the time, and I'm not just talking about the complaints from the women."

I knew what she was talking about as we had the same problems in the military.

Thirty minutes later we managed to find our way back to the large breakfast buffet at the front of the ship. If something had happened onboard, you couldn't tell it from the mass of passengers going about the daily shipboard activity of eating too much. I wondered if my imagination was getting to me, but my worry that something bad had happened didn't want to go away.

"These little pastries are pretty good," I said, mostly to make conversation as Rose appeared to be distracted.

A group of teenage girls stood up and left the table next to us. "Did you see what they were doing?" Rose asked.

"No."

"They were passing around and sharing their mascara."

"Okay," I said, but I knew I was missing something.

She scrunched her face. "It's not very sanitary. I know a lot of girls do it, but I don't like it. Lipstick, chap stick, even toothbrushes, yuck."

I nodded and looked at the departing teenagers in a show of support for Rose's opinion. In reality, I didn't care to think much about the hygiene habits of teenagers.

"Looks like we're coming into the harbor," I said.

"I've never seen anything like this. We should be out on the deck," Rose said, standing up to get a better look out the windows.

"I think we have plenty of time to finish eating and still get out there to watch the ship come to a stop. I don't know if we anchor or tie up to a dock somewhere. It's been a while since I've been to Cozumel, and all these places are a little different."

Rose sat back down. "Okay, but I want to see how they park this thing."

As I expected, the ship hadn't come to a stop by the time we finished eating. We started walking out of the dining room and passed Matt and Dylan sitting together a row over from the aisle we had taken.

"Hey, guys," Rose called out.

They both looked up and nodded. Matt included a slight hand gesture, but neither said anything that might indicate they wanted us to stop and visit. We kept walking, and Rose leaned in close to me.

"Not very friendly this morning."

"They looked preoccupied," I said.

"Still," she said without elaboration.

Up on the top deck, we stood close to the rail and watched everything transpire as the ship moved into a slot along a long pier.

"I can't imagine trying to parallel park this giant thing," Rose said.

"It must take a lot of practice. I wonder if they have ships that can park themselves, like those new cars that I see in those commercials. You know, where the car parks itself."

"I've seen them. One day, this world will get to a point where we won't have to do anything, because technology will do it all for us. I wonder how you fire someone then. I mean, if you're the guy or gal in charge of some robot that is supposed to make something, and the thing isn't made right, do you fire the robot or the person in charge? It would only make sense that you'd fire the robot, but if that's the case, why have the human at all?"

"Who knows," I said, not really following who was firing whom. "My bigger concern is if we make the robots smart enough, they may wonder why they need to put up with humans."

"Hopefully, none of that will happen in our lifetime. I have enough trouble remembering my passwords."

"I think we're stopped and docked," I said. "I suggest we find a restaurant, have lunch in Cozumel, do a little walking around, and maybe some shopping. What would you like to do?"

"Oh, I don't care what we do, but I do want to walk around a little." She looked down at the long concrete pier below. "When will they start letting people off?"

"I don't know, but fairly soon I would think."

"I can't decide if I should buy some gifts for my nieces and nephews. I'd like to, but I have so many of them."

"If you buy them tee shirts, it won't take up too much room in the suitcase or in a bag." I figured she was worried more about carrying a bunch of things around and back home than the cost.

"That may be a good idea and should prevent any of them from getting upset by thinking someone else got the better present. How about you, Jim, you need to get anything?"

"No, I just need to buy you something."

"No you don't. Besides if you buy me something, I'll have to buy you something, so we should just buy something for ourselves."

"Okay," I said, but I wondered if this was one of those times when a guy wasn't supposed to listen to his gal. As for me, I didn't want anything from Cozumel or anyplace else. "I guess I could take a dog toy home for Chubbs."

Rose put her hand around mine and squeezed. "That's sweet. I bet he misses you when you're gone."

"Oh, I don't know. The neighbor kids keep him busy. He's normally worn out when I get home."

"When do I get to meet him?"

"That's a tough question. Taking a lady friend home to meet the dog is getting pretty serious, don't you think?"

"Oh, I don't know. It can't be too much more serious than

taking me on this cruise," she said with a grin that dared me to argue with her.

"He'll love you," I said, and I meant it, but I also felt like the fish that suddenly discovers a hook set in its jaw.

"Whatever the problem is or was that caused the crew to close off one side of the ship earlier hasn't seemed to affect our schedule," Rose said.

"No matter what it was, I can see why the cruise line doesn't want to interrupt the schedule or interfere with the plans of thousands of its passengers. Besides they should be able to fix whatever it was by the time we leave tonight."

Chapter 9

"Are you surprised we haven't seen your friend Sarah or her friends?" Rose asked as we left the restaurant after having a late lunch on shore.

Cozumel's main street ran along the waterfront and streamed with pedestrian traffic. The sun beat down on us, making it feel more like midsummer than late fall. Rose wore white shorts and a sleeveless pink blouse. She looked really good, and I was happy that unless someone knew it, no one would ever guess that a few months earlier, she had nearly died from a gunshot that tried to take the top of her head off.

"No, not really. I mean we did see two of the guys having breakfast, and here on the island there are a lot of people from our ship, and there's at least one other cruise ship here today, too. Besides, they might have all finally agreed to go on one of the excursions."

She nodded. "I hope everything has calmed down between the bride and groom. I can't imagine that it's any fun being stuck together on a ship with someone you're angry with, even if you're recently married."

"I don't know how anyone could be angry with Sarah," I said and tried to hide my grin.

"I've always thought it's funny how guys who get dumped," she may have emphasized dumped a little more than necessary, "by old girlfriends continue to carry the torch for them so long." She didn't try to hide her grin.

"You're loving this, aren't you," I said.

"Yep."

Three Americans who may have had too much to drink walked by us causing us to step to the edge of the road.

"This sidewalk is crowded. I wonder what it's like when the ships aren't here."

"I imagine that's when the locals do their shopping," she said. "Unless you want to stop somewhere else, I suggest we head back to the ship. I think I'd like to lie out in this sun for a while."

"Let's do it," I said.

"You could use a little sun yourself."

"I know it." Actually, I had a pretty good farmer's, or maybe I should say golfer's tan.

The line to get back on the ship was longer and moved slower than I remembered from earlier cruises. When we reached the security processing area, I saw why.

Two security personnel aimed a video camera on a tri-pod at the returning passengers. Positioned beyond the conveyor belt that x-rayed the contents of any carry on items, the video camera captured everyone coming back on board. Additionally, rather than simply look at our cruise ID card and let us on, other security personnel asked each of us where we were from and annotated it in the computer.

"That was odd," I said when we were on the elevator heading up to our room.

"I'm not familiar with the process, Jim, but I definitely got the idea that they are looking for something or someone."

"I agree."

"I wonder if we'll ever get to know what's going on?" she asked.

"Probably not, but I can't imagine it'll have much of an impact on us either." We took a crowded elevator up to our deck. "I think I'm ready for a nap," I said when we reached our cabin.

"I thought we were going to lie out by the pool and catch some sun."

"Oh yeah," I said, having totally forgotten her earlier remark, "but don't let me fall asleep out there, or I'll burn up."

"Hey, it looks like we have a message," Rose pointed at the phone on the desk.

"Probably some announcement about our departure time," I said and started to get undressed, ignoring the flashing light.

Rose picked up the receiver and pushed a button on the cradle. She gave me a funny look. "Here, you better listen to this. Sounds like your old girlfriend is upset about something and wants her old boyfriend back."

"What are you talking about?"

She held out the phone for me.

"Should we act like we never got the message?" I asked.

"No, she seems a bit frantic."

I took the phone, and after Rose pushed the button to repeat the message, listened.

The voice on the phone belonged to Sarah, but the words came out between sobs and were hard to understand. "Jim, I need to see you, something terrible happened, and I don't know what to do. He's gone..." I couldn't understand what she said for about a half a sentence. "Something terrible. I need you ..." Again the sobs interfered with her speech, and then the call ended.

"What do you think is going on?" Rose asked.

"I have no idea. I couldn't even understand everything she said. What do you think?"

"I don't know either, but I do know that I didn't come on this cruise to share your time with one of your old girlfriends. I have absolutely no problem with your going to talk to her, but that's it. Give her some sage advice about life and relationships and then come back here, and we don't see them again."

"I don't want to go alone. I'm thinking maybe they got into an argument, and he beat her up. You need to come with me."

"Okay, I didn't want you to go alone anyway," she smiled. "This is crazy, though. What does she expect us to do? She has a bunch of friends with her on the cruise. Can't they rally around her? You know, I didn't get the impression they were big fans of Joe anyway."

"They weren't. Something about this I don't like," I said but kept my thoughts to myself.

"Same here. Time does things to people's minds, and maybe she's built you up into some super hero or Zen sex master or something."

"What? That's silly."

"Believe me, my thoughts exactly," she said and looked away from me. "I just don't like this."

Rather than continue repeating how much we didn't like the situation, I put my shirt back on, and we left in search of Sarah's cabin.

When we reached her hallway, we noticed a lone ship's officer sitting on a chair outside a room in front of us.

"What do you bet that that's her cabin," Rose said.

"I imagine you're right."

The ship's officer, a burly guy with a red beard and a name tag that read O'Malley stood when we approached him. He must have thought we would walk right by him, because we surprised him when we asked him if Sarah or Joe Lassiter were in the room.

Rather than answer the question, he asked us his own question. "What business do you have with them?" I thought he started to say her instead of them.

"She called and asked us to come to her room," Rose said. "What's going on?"

"Stay here," he said, and after sliding a key card in the reader on the door, he stuck his head in the room. "Did you ask for anyone to come visit you?"

She said something, and as O'Malley pulled his head back, I heard Sarah call out. "Jim, Jim is that you?"

O'Malley took his six foot plus frame away from the door as Sarah opened it.

"Please, come in."

If she was upset with seeing Rose with me, I couldn't tell, and Rose didn't hesitate before entering the cabin on my heels.

"I'm glad you came, Rose, Joe's been murdered."

There it was. No preamble or build up, just the statement that Joe had been murdered.

"What? How?" Rose asked, echoing my feelings.

I looked closer at Sarah. Her eyes looked moist but didn't start tearing up.

"I'm so sorry," Rose said. She gave Sarah a hug and looked back at me like I needed to do something.

I stepped in when Rose released her and hugged Sarah. "Are you alright?" I asked while we were still hugging.

"Of course she's not alright," Rose answered for her. "The man she married a couple of days ago is dead."

"It's okay, Rose," Sarah said. "No, Jim, I'm not alright. I'm not physically damaged, if that's what you mean, but I feel all broken up inside. I'm glad you came. I'm glad both of you came. I need someone to talk to, and my friends are supportive and sweet, but they want to keep saying everything will be okay. I need to know what happened and why. I know we may never know, but I can't sit here simply thinking that everything will be ok, because it won't. Someone killed my husband." A tear escaped from an eye, and she reached up, wiping it away with the back of her hand.

"I couldn't either, and I don't think anyone else could accept the remark that it will be okay as a solution," Rose said.

"What have they told you?" I asked.

"Not a lot." She paused for a moment like she was gathering her thoughts. "They found Joe last night or early this morning but before sunrise. They found him out on the promenade on Deck 5, where I left him."

"You left him, when?" I asked, even though I knew Joe was not with her when we saw her the night before.

"We had a little spat. He had been acting a little strange ever since we boarded."

"Strange? In what way?" I asked.

"Just personal things, and like last night, you know, like we said last night, he didn't want to go to the show with the rest of us. But nothing that gave me any clue he was worried about anything, if that's what you mean?"

"Okay," I said.

"You know on the fifth deck they have that area where you can stand outside and look at the water. I think you can walk all the way around the ship on that deck. They found him out there. Someone had stabbed him in the back." Sarah paused for a moment like she was trying to gather her thoughts. "They said he died instantly."

"Who's investigating his murder?" Rose asked.

"I don't know. I mean the ship's security personnel are, but I don't know if they call someone in to help. Who would they call?"

"Good question," I said. "Tell us what you know, from the beginning. What time did you leave him out there?"

"It was just after dark. We had all eaten dinner in the main restaurant and were slowly making our way to the theater. He said he didn't want to go. I followed him out to the deck and tried to talk him into coming with us. No one else came out with me, and I didn't see anyone else out there. They asked me that, so I thought I would tell you, too. It makes me a suspect, of course, but I didn't do it."

"I believe you," I said.

During my days as an investigator, I had always felt that saying you believed someone who was discussing a crime they may have committed or was involved in was a good way to keep them talking, even if you didn't really believe them. In this case, though, I believed her.

She smiled. "I didn't see anyone else out on the deck when I left him to join the others. I thought he might change his mind and show up at the theater, but he didn't. After the show, I called the room, but he didn't answer. They think he was already dead by then. Then we ran into you two at the lounge."

"How long did you stay at the lounge?" I asked.

"Only about a half hour after you left. We were all exhausted. When I got to my cabin, I was surprised he wasn't there. He's not a late night person."

"What did you do?" I asked.

"That's just it, I didn't do anything. I didn't even try to stay awake. I know I should've, but I was really angry at him, and I had no inkling of an idea that something may have happened to him. This morning, around six, they came knocking on my door."

"They?" Rose asked.

"The ship's security personnel. At first they were real aloof, asking me questions about Joe. I went from thinking he got into a fight with someone to thinking he fell overboard. They finally told me he had been killed, and they needed me to identify the body."

"I hope they let you call someone to go with you," Rose said.

"No, they said they would accompany me and time was important. They took me down to deck one and then to a small room where they had him. It was him. They said it took them over an hour to identify him. They had to go through all the pictures they take when you board. Someone had taken his wallet, and his room key was missing."

"What did they tell you had happened?" I asked.

"Not much more than what I've already said."

"Did you see the wound?" I asked.

She shook her head. "The captain stopped by before I left the room where they had him. He remembered that he had married us and wanted to tell me how sorry he was. He said they would do everything they could to find out who killed Joe. He looked really affected by it."

"I imagine he was," Rose said.

"But they still interrogated me like they thought I had done it."

"When was that?" I asked.

"A few minutes after I identified the body and the captain left, they took me into another room. At first, they were real nice and brought me coffee and water. I signed a form acknowledging who I was and that I recognized Joe. Then, they left me alone for a few minutes, before two of them came back in and started asking me questions." She paused for a moment, perhaps to allow us to ask any questions, but Rose and I remained silent. "That's when the real interrogation took place. Where had I been last night, who was with me, when was the last time I saw Joe, why he wasn't with me, had we been having problems, and so on."

"Did they seem to accept your answers?" Rose asked.

"I think so. I started crying, of course, and I guess that may have helped. Plus, the fact that I had nothing to do with his death helped."

"What else did they ask you?" I wanted to learn more about their questions. In doing so, I thought it could help me see what gaps they might have in their investigation, and possibly, what they already knew.

"They wanted to know if Joe or I had brought a knife or large scissors onto the ship. Of course we hadn't. They asked what might have been in his wallet, and one of them told me if we shared the same credit cards, I needed to cancel all of them. We'd only just got married, so we hadn't combined any accounts yet. They wanted to know who else Joe knew on the cruise. I told them besides the wedding party, there was no one. I didn't even remember he met you two."

"Well, I imagine they'll want to talk to us now, so we can set that record straight," Rose said.

"Did you get the impression that they had the murder weapon?" I asked.

"They didn't show me anything to identify. If I had to guess,

I'd say that they hadn't found it yet. They did ask me if we had been arguing about anything. I made a mistake there by saying our whole first couple of days married had not been perfect. Something had been bothering him, or at least he hadn't been acting like the Joe I thought I knew."

"What do you mean?" I asked.

"That's what they asked. Joe had become demanding, a bit arrogant, and assumed that I was supposed to do whatever he said. It didn't make sense to me. I've known him for seven months, and he had never been like that before. Oh, they asked one question that I thought was odd. They wanted to know where Joe and I were the night before he was killed."

"Did they explain why?" Rose asked.

"No, and they accepted my answer without any follow up or clarification."

"Why is there someone outside your door?" I asked.

"They said it was to keep people from bothering me. I can leave whenever I want. The truth is I don't want to go anywhere except home."

We talked a little longer and tried to be as supportive as possible. Before we left her, Rose asked the question that I'd been avoiding. "Do you want us to try to find his killer?"

"Yes," Sarah said, and while she looked at Rose when she said this, her eyes moved to mine, and I could see the plea for help as clearly as I could see the tears that now dripped from them.

Chapter 10

"I know you didn't want me to ask that question," Rose said once we were out of the room.

"About trying to find her husband's killer?"

"Yes. Couldn't you see that was what she wanted all along?"

"But how are we supposed to do it on a ship. It's huge. We've been lost twice on this ship already," I grinned at her, since both times were caused by her insistence on our going in a certain direction that turned out wrong.

"I know, but this is different. I'll introduce us to the captain and tell him I'm a homicide detective and you're a famous police consultant. They can't have anyone on the crew who is experienced in handling homicides."

"I think you might be stretching our credentials a little. A famous police consultant? I'm not even an ordinary police consultant. In fact, I'm not a consultant of any type."

"Then how should I refer to you when I'm trying to impress the captain?"

"If we have to go through with this, tell him I'm a nice guy who shouldn't mess up his investigation too much."

"If we stick to the truth, the captain will never allow either of us to tag along," Rose said. "My own boss doesn't even want me back on the job."

"Well, we both know he's an idiot, and I think he's a little jealous about the nice citation you got from the FBI, and all the press you received."

"Yeah, all for getting shot in the head, nothing else."

"You know you're wrong there, Rose. If I remember right, it was you who developed the rapport with the young kid that gave us the big breaks in the case. The FBI had all but given up on finding that briefcase."

"All I can see us doing is offering advice to whoever is running the investigation."

"If they let us," I said.

"But why wouldn't they?"

"Pride, ego, distrust, fear of being second guessed, loss of control, I could go on."

"I imagine the cruise line will want to keep a lid on this as long as they can," Rose said.

"They might already be paranoid a little, seeing as how they should have discovered by now that Sarah is a reporter. Being sued is one thing, but having the fact that people are being murdered on your cruise line blasted all over the New York prime time news is a whole different matter."

"See, they need us," Rose said.

I didn't see her logic, but I kept that to myself. "So, what do you recommend for our first step?"

"Should we make a direct approach to the captain?" she asked.

"We could, but if he says no, we may be dead in the water, excuse the pun. I suggest we start with the chief of security. That way if he doesn't want us, we can still go to the captain of the ship."

"Sounds like a plan. Do we approach the reception desk and ask to speak to someone from security?"

"That may be the most effective way, or we could just ask

her." I pointed to the tall blonde whom I recognized as Inga, the ship's officer who had told me earlier in the day that part of the ship was off limits.

"Because she's part of the crew, or because she happens to be very pretty?"

"She's the ship's officer whom I told you about. The one who didn't let me go out onto the deck today."

"Oh the 'just some crewperson' you mentioned," she said, giving me a stern look. "Wipe that silly grin off your face."

"I think she recognizes me," I said. "Let's go talk to her."

Inga did smile and wave at me, while she talked to someone through a hand held device that reminded me of the old walkie-talkies. Rose raised an eyebrow that I read as 'how well do you know this woman?'

I felt my ego climb a few levels as we approached Inga. It dropped just as quickly when another ship's officer appeared next to her and called out my name.

"Mr. West?" he said.

I nodded.

"I'm Johann Needles. The captain has requested that I have a few words with you. Could you come with me?" He gestured with an open palm to his left. His accent was Northern European, but his English was good. He stood a good two inches taller than me, and because of his blond hair, I thought he might have been one of the three ship's officers I saw that morning.

I glanced over and saw more of the ship's crew standing about fifteen feet away. Unlike Inga and Needles, these two were dressed in the white attire worn by the many crew personnel who did the manual labor around the ship.

"Go ahead and go with him, Jim. I'll be alright here with Inga."

I imagined this was Rose's way of telling me this might be our way into the investigation, or of course, she could just be throwing me under the bus. My bet was on the former. While she saw an opportunity, I saw that I was being led off to be interrogated. I wondered if these modern day ships still had people walk the plank.

The two crewmen, Officer Needles, and I took an elevator into the bowels of the ship. No one said anything on the elevator. Once off, Needles led me to a small room furnished only with a wooden table and two chairs. It smelled of an air freshener, and I wondered why. He gestured for me to go inside. I did, and in a move that kind of surprised me, he shut the door behind me and left me alone in the room.

I sat down in the chair that faced the door and glanced around the small room. Other than a small black, inverted dome attached to the ceiling that I guessed hid a camera, I didn't see anything else, not even some dust on the floor.

Taking my phone out of my pocket, I started playing solitaire. I did it for a couple of reasons. First, I knew their curiosity to find out what I was doing on my phone might cut down my wait time. I also wanted to give them the impression, once they saw what I was doing, that I wasn't concerned about the interview.

After about five minutes, Officer Needles came back into the room. He carried a three ring binder much like I used in college a couple decades ago.

"First, I want to thank you for coming with us. I'm sure you know by now we had a serious crime committed on board this ship last night," he said.

"Yes, I'm aware someone murdered Joe Lassiter."

"What do you know about it?" he asked.

"Other than that, almost nothing." I thought about passing the lead back to him, but I realized my answer only begged for closure. "I understand that he was stabbed in the back, that his wallet is missing, and that someone discovered him during the night outside on the fifth deck. That's it."

"How well did you know Mr. Lassiter?"

"Didn't know him at all. Only met him once on the ship, and I may have exchanged a handful of words with him, but that's all."

"How well do you know his wife?"

"I met her several years ago. We became close friends over a period of a week or two, but we haven't spent any time together or even been in contact much since. I didn't know she was going to be on this cruise."

For the next ten minutes, I answered questions about my past, the reasons I signed up for the cruise, my movements since boarding and other general, irrelevant topics. In a response to my question, Needles described his position on the ship as deputy chief of operations. As such, the ship's security fell under him, or more correctly, under his boss and then the captain.

"Why do you think someone murdered Lassiter?" he finally got around to asking.

"I haven't the slightest idea."

"Do you think his wife might have murdered him?"

"I don't think so," I said. "Unless she has changed drastically, the Sarah I knew was too tough of a woman to ever have to resort to murder."

He raised his right eyebrow, perhaps for some elaboration, but I didn't go on.

"Any reason to believe one of the wedding party could have done it?" he asked.

"I don't know them well enough to say either way."

A knock on the door interrupted us. He went to answer it and then stepped outside. Ten minutes passed before he returned.

"Mr. West, something has come to our attention that we need to digest for a while. Can we resume this discussion later today?"

"Of course. Hopefully not back here, though."

"I'll see what I can do," he said. While he escorted me all the way to the elevators, he did not get on with me.

I took the elevators to the eighth deck and returned to our cabin not knowing what was going on or how Needles planned to make contact later in the day. While it didn't surprise me that Rose wasn't in the room, I did wonder what she was up to and if I should remain in the room to wait for her.

I collapsed on the bed and tried to focus my mind on things other than Sarah and her murdered husband of what, two days? I didn't have much success and didn't like the thought that I was losing control over what I had hoped to be a relaxing and enjoyable cruise with Rose.

As if to highlight my lack of control, the face of Joe Lassiter popped into my mind, and I wondered why someone murdered him.

Seventeen years earlier, I had a not so different of a case of my own. An air force master sergeant and his new bride had travelled from their honeymoon to report for duty in the weather squadron at Offutt AFB, Nebraska. The couple moved into base housing, and a few nights later, a neighbor found the master sergeant dead in his backyard. The neighbor called for an ambulance and the police, before he proceeded with his wife to knock on the victim's front door. The neighbor's wife was certain the dead master sergeant's new wife had been home all day.

The victim's wife answered the door and appeared shocked when she heard the news. She had been inside watching television. The neighbor and his wife believed her reaction was authentic. A polygraph of the victim's wife two days later supported her innocence. Sensing right away that she was a prime suspect, she had requested a polygraph, which she passed.

The master sergeant died from a bullet wound to the head. In our investigation, we didn't find any weapon in or around the house, nor did any of the neighbors hear a gunshot. The victim didn't appear to have any enemies, and for several days, the investigation went nowhere.

By chance, we learned the Omaha police had responded to a call about a shot being fired on the same evening the sergeant died. When the police arrived at the scene not far from the air base, they discovered two men who had detained four young teenagers. The teenagers admitted to the police that they had been playing around with one of the teenager's father's old, war souvenir pistol. They thought the pistol was empty. One of the kids pulled the trigger. The pistol fired a round that scared the teenagers and drew the ire of two adults talking nearby.

Despite the astronomical odds against it, we eventually determined that the round from that weapon killed the master sergeant in his backyard nearly a third of a mile away.

I wondered why that memory came back to me, other than the thought that once your time is up, it's up. Maybe Lassiter had been killed for no reason other than somebody wanted to kill someone. If that was the case, barring any break in security video coverage or an unexpected evidence find, his killer would likely never be identified.

Chapter 11

The smug look on Rose's face when she entered our room a few minutes later told me that she had successfully maneuvered our way into the investigation. I was less than thrilled.

"How'd it go?" she asked me.

"Not too bad. They didn't get me to confess if that's what you mean, but I didn't learn anything either. I take it you succeeded in getting us involved."

She nodded, still grinning.

"You know, you're a lot more excited about this than I am," I said.

"I told the captain that there were no guarantees."

"You saw the captain?"

"Yes," her grin actually widened. "Captain Niemann. He's handsome."

I wanted to make some witty comeback, but settled on ignoring the comment. "How involved are we?"

"They want us to assist them. While they may well keep a few things to themselves, the captain has instructed his staff to take advantage of our expertise. To quote him the best I can recall, he told Jerry Bergren 'to take advantage of our experience and our familiarity with the victim and his associates,' or something like that."

"Is Bergren in charge of security?"

"I think he's like the number two on this ship, but I got the impression the security division falls under him. He wants to meet with both of us in," she looked at her watch, "about an hour. Oh, and guess what?"

"Bergren is handsome, too?"

"Maybe in a rugged way," she teased. "You were right. Yesterday morning's incident may have been connected to Lassiter's murder."

"How?"

"They didn't elaborate, but I think they will. The captain said that two men have been killed the same way on this cruise, and that they needed help in getting to the bottom of all this. That seemed to be the main reason he was accepting my offer, two murders the same way."

I thought about that for a second. "If we have a serial killer who has done these without any personal connection to the dead men, there's little chance anyone will catch the killer unless he screws up, and they won't need our help if that happens."

"I believe Captain Niemann and Bergren have already come to that conclusion, and they are desperate," Rose said.

"If I was in charge of the cruise line, I'd be sending in experts of my own."

"They may be doing that, but it could take a couple of days for anyone to reach the boat."

"By then the cruise will be over," I said.

She nodded. "How sure are you that Sarah isn't our killer?"

"Of both men?"

"Of either," she said.

"One hundred percent."

"How about someone in her party?"

"No idea," I said.

"If the timelines of the killings are correct, they all seem to have alibis unless they were doing it as couples or a group."

"By doing it, I hope you mean the murders."

"Yes, Jim, anything else they want to do as couples or in a group is none of our business and nothing I want to think about. And, for the record, I don't think anyone in the group is involved with either of the murders. The fact that the murders were done in the same way does seem to link the two incidents."

"I agree. Did they elaborate in what they meant when they told you the two were killed in the same way?"

"No, but if they want our help, they'll have to tell us."

I nodded. "By the way, I can see how they agreed to your helping them, but how did you get them to agree to my involvement?"

"When I pitched my offer to your friend Inga, I gave her a few internet links to look at. I did this right after you left."

"Oh," I said, not all that thrilled with them reading about me. "Some of the things written about me out there are not very accurate."

"I only gave them a few. The ones I like, and of course, Sarah's long article she wrote years back."

I wondered by the way she said "Sarah's long article" meant she didn't care for it.

"Despite that article being a little gushy, I think that was the one that got their interest. You give them an inside look at Sarah and her friends. They don't know any better, so if I was them, I would look at you as an insider."

"Hardly," I said.

"They probably jumped to the conclusion that Sarah and her friends might tell you things that they wouldn't tell them. It's fairly sound logic."

"But, using the same logic, they might think telling us what they know could be counterproductive. They may think we would run right back and tell the group everything they're doing in the investigation."

"I know," Rose said. "It's a tradeoff. However, my guess is that they have very little, if anything, to run with right now and aren't worried about keeping any big secrets from us."

"Well, we can sit around here guessing or do something productive in the short time we have before we have to go to our meeting. How about we go get a coke or an ice cream or something?"

"An ice cream treat sounds perfectly productive. I wonder if they have banana splits on this ship," she said.

We found the ice cream parlor without much trouble, since we had walked by it on one of our walks around the ship. I ordered a diet coke and we shared a banana split. Rose didn't order a drink, but ended up sharing my diet coke. Surprisingly, we didn't talk about the murders or Sarah and her friends.

After finishing the banana split, we went up to the top deck and watched the line of passengers return to the ship.

"I guess we'll be leaving soon," I said.

"Do you remember what time the ship is supposed to leave?"

"No, I heard them announce it, but I wasn't paying attention. If I remember right, we are usually out at sea for dinner, so I imagine we should be leaving by five."

As we watched, a smaller boat carrying a few dozen rowdy passengers maneuvered around our ship and pulled up to a docking station on the long pier. A few minutes later, its passengers disembarked the boat and joined the constant stream of people returning to our ship. A number of those getting off the boat appeared to have had a little too much to drink and had difficulty walking in a straight line or at a steady pace.

"Looks like they might have had a good time somewhere," Rose said.

"I wonder if that's the party boat excursion. I think it goes off to some deserted beach and sets up a picnic with a lot of cheap booze."

"Might have been fun ten years ago," Rose said,

"My thoughts exactly. My love for hangovers left me long ago."

We strolled around to the other side of the ship and watched as a few ships passed by. We could see the Mexican mainland in the distance.

Glancing at her watch, Rose said, "Guess we ought to head to our meeting. It's about that time." Despite her comment, she didn't move away from the rail. "Maybe we shouldn't have stuck our noses into all this."

I wanted to say "We?"

Instead, I said, "It wouldn't be that hard to gracefully bow out. We could offer some advice and express a willingness to talk to the wedding party and report back. Limit what they expect from us."

"What about Sarah?"

"I can't believe she really expects us to solve the murder."

"I know," Rose said, "but let's go meet with whoever is in charge of this investigation and see if they will even share what they have with us. If they don't, we'll be in a much better position to back out."

She led me down to the deck where we had first entered the

ship, and we approached a large counter, behind which stood three sharply dressed crew members. These three seemed occupied answering questions posed by passengers who formed a line with at least a dozen people in it. Rose started to get in line, when I noticed Inga motioning to us from a doorway behind the counter.

"I think we've been invited back there," I said to Rose and nodded my head toward Inga.

We walked around the counter and approached Inga.

"Follow me, please," she said.

I did like that accent.

She took us down a hall and into a large office that contained a rectangular table that could easily sit eight people.

"Please take a chair, they will be with you in a minute," she said and left the room.

The minute turned out to be more like ten seconds. Inga had barely left when four men entered the room. Rose and I stood.

"Glad you could make it, Deputy Luna, and you must be Mr. West," the man with the most gold bars on his uniform said. "I'm Jerry Bergren." He stood about my height, a shade over six feet, and I put him around my age, but whereas a little grey was showing up in my hair, his hair was jet black.

I accepted his outstretched hand and said, "Please call me Jim."

"Let's all sit down," Jerry said. "I must admit when the idea of you two helping us in this investigation was first suggested to me, I didn't like the idea. However, after conversations with the skipper and our corporate offices, it made more sense, and I mean just that. I oversee all operations on this ship, and that includes ship security, but I'll be the first to admit we're not really trained or equipped to handle this."

While he talked, two men worked on setting up a large monitor at one end of the table which they plugged into a laptop.

"As you know, the cruise will be over in a couple of days. That gives us an almost impossible task of identifying the murderer before all the passengers leave the ship. I realize the killer may not be a passenger, but the departure of nearly three quarters of our potential suspects will significantly undermine the investigation."

"Can any help be sent in to assist you?" I asked.

"Yes, but the soonest they can get here is late tomorrow."

"We're ready," one of the men who set up the monitor and laptop said.

"Thanks. I just need one of you to stay in case I mess up," Jerry said.

The younger looking of the two stayed.

"By the way, this is Henri. Don't try to pronounce his last name. We all just call him Henri," Jerry grinned at his partner sitting next to him.

I had already noticed his last name from his nametag on his uniform. It started with a P and had at least a dozen letters in it. He also had one of the shiniest bald heads I had ever seen.

"Henri," Rose said in acknowledgement and smiled. "I'm Rose."

Henri smiled back at Rose. He and I nodded at each other.

"We've decided to bring you fully into this. All I need is your word that you will not share what we tell you with outsiders, and that you both will keep us informed of everything you find that may be of help to us in the investigation." Jerry looked at both of us.

"You've got our word," Rose said.

He looked at me.

"Mine, too."

"During each of the past two nights, we've had someone killed in the same manner and by whom we believe is the same person. Two nights ago, it was a crewman. At that point we thought the killer had to be another crewman. It's not uncommon to have fights among some of the members of the crew, and we could see no reason for a passenger to kill him."

"Makes sense," I said.

"Last night's incident turned our theory on its head. It also changed the level of urgency to get this matter resolved. While we certainly don't approve of anyone killing anyone on this ship, one crewman killing another is something we can handle over time, and to be frank, we can keep out of the headlines. This second murder shocked us. It throws everything we thought about the first one overboard. The two victims have nothing in common. The first victim was a poor kid from the Philippines. The second was a rich young man from New York who has, as far as we can tell, never been to the Philippines. This second murder opens up the possibility that anyone on the ship could be the killer, and it puts us on a deadline to solve it." After Jerry said this, he stood up and walked over to a corner of the room to a coffee pot that I hadn't noticed when we entered the room.

"Coffee, anyone?" he asked after he had poured a cup.

I looked at Rose who shook her head. "I'll have one," I said and walked over to the pot.

Jerry offered me the cup he had in his hand and poured another cup for himself. I thanked him, and we returned to the table.

"I can continue, but do you have any questions?" Jerry asked.

"What convinced you the same person committed both murders?" Rose asked.

"The same weapon, a sharp bladed weapon, killed both individuals, and both victims were stabbed in the exact same spot." He reached up and touched a spot behind his neck. "Right here."

"One stab wound each?" Rose asked.

"Yes, the killer knew what he was doing."

"Did he leave behind any message, note, or any other kind of calling card?" she asked.

"No."

"Any security camera coverage?"

"Not of the first murder. That was one of the reasons we thought it was done by a member of the crew. We do have a number of security cameras around the ship, but the one in that area has not worked for a while. Fixing it had not been a priority," Jerry said.

"That means you have some coverage of the second incident," I said.

"Yes," he turned and looked at the man at the end of the table.

The man had not been introduced to us, but Jerry must not have felt it was necessary.

"The security footage?" the man asked.

"Yes."

The monitor came to life and in a few seconds we were watching a grainy, dark recording of the outside deck where Lassiter was killed. At first I didn't see anyone, but then a man came out onto the deck. The low quality of the video prevented me from recognizing the person.

"That's Lassiter," Jerry said. "No one else is out on the deck.

In a few seconds you'll see his wife come out and join him. We have not done anything to speed up what you're seeing, so the time lapse is just what it is." Another person came out the same door and walked directly to Lassiter.

"That's Sarah," Rose said.

"Yes," Jerry agreed.

We watched as Sarah and Joe appeared to have a brief conversation. Sarah left, and Joe drifted farther toward the back of the ship and toward the camera.

"In just a minute we'll see our killer," Jerry said.

"Is this the best quality you have?" I asked.

"Unfortunately, yes. We sent a copy off to see if we can get it enhanced, but I'm not too optimistic. Here comes our man."

A person whom I couldn't be sure was even a man walked out onto the deck through the same door. He paused for a moment at the railing before casually walking toward Lassiter.

"He's wearing slacks and a baseball cap. He keeps his head turned down slightly."

"Is he wearing glasses?" Rose asked.

"Yes, good catch, Deputy. It took us a couple times reviewing this before we caught that. As you can see, he walks right up to Lassiter. He never looks up. We don't know if he is doing that to keep his face hidden from any surveillance cameras or from Lassiter. Once he meets up with our victim, our view of his face is blocked by Lassiter."

"Lassiter looks a little bigger than him," Rose said.

"Like he's two or three inches taller," Henri joined the conversation.

The two men on the screen appeared to have a short conversation. Neither displayed any animation that might indicate they were quarreling. We watched as the killer pointed to something on the floor of the deck near the wall of the ship. They talked for a second longer, and then Lassiter leaned over like he might be picking up whatever they were looking at. As he leans over, he goes out of view of the camera. The killer moves over a little behind him and also goes out of view. Suddenly, at the bottom of the screen an arm swings in an arc.

"Stop there and go back a second to where the arm first appears," Jerry said.

The screen flashed to the arm paused in the air. In the man's hand was an object.

"The best we can tell is that it's a bladed weapon. We can't make out a handle, but we're certain it is the murder weapon." Jerry turned to the man operating the laptop. "Okay, let it continue."

We watched as the killer stands up with his back to us and walks away. After taking a couple of steps and without breaking stride, he throws a couple of items overboard. He doesn't go inside through the doors he used earlier but continues on toward a set of doors farther down.

The screen goes blank.

"Any coverage of him coming in or leaving the interior of the ship?" I asked.

"Only a quick sideways shot of him going into the restroom next to the casino. Can you pull that up?" Jerry asked.

The computer guy punched a key or two and a still picture appeared on the monitor. At first, I couldn't make heads or tails out of what I was seeing other than a crowd of people. Jerry stood up and leaned toward the screen, touching a spot on the top left with his pen.

"Right there."

"Good catch," Rose said.

I stared at the monitor and finally saw a man in a ball cap about to go into what I imagined was the restroom.

"This camera covers a section of the casino. It's only by chance it caught him. As you can see, it's not a very good shot. We can tell he's Caucasian, wears glasses, and there's no indication of any facial hair. He's wearing slacks of some sort and a dark, long sleeve shirt. Doesn't seem to be carrying anything."

"Can you enhance that?" Rose asked.

"This is enhanced, but like I said, we've sent a copy off so the experts can play with it."

"How about when he comes out?" Rose asked.

"We don't have him coming out. I don't mean he didn't, but on a few occasions after he goes in, groups of people gather or pass through that area blocking the view. We believe he came out during one of those periods of time. By the time we saw this, the cleaning crews had been in and out of that restroom three times."

"I take it you've looked at other camera footage to try to find him," I said.

"Yes, and we're still looking. While we have several security cameras, we don't have them set up to watch every part of the ship. Some of the newer ships are better equipped, but even then, it would take hundreds of cameras to adequately cover a ship of this size." Jerry looked at us and waited a second for us to ask another question. When we didn't, he looked back at the man controlling the computer. "Let's show them the picture of the two victims' wounds side by side."

The screen flashed to a picture of the upper backs of the two victims. Both had a nasty gash at the base of their necks.

"That's where the blade penetrated the victims. Same size wounds and both stabbed at nearly the same spot. Even the depth of both wounds is similar."

"He knew what he was doing," I said.

"We wondered about that. Could he be a doctor? Who else would know that a deep enough puncture there would sever the brain stem? Could he be a serial killer who has learned this over time? These are just some of the possibilities we have discussed," Jerry said.

"I imagine death occurred pretty quickly in each case?" Rose asked.

"Yes, very little blood. Both victims fell face down. We did not find a weapon at either scene."

"The baseball hat is fairly distinctive. You don't have any other security footage of a man walking around with that hat on at any other time on the cruise?" Rose asked.

I bit my lip and let Jerry answer her question.

"Because of the sunshine on cruises, we find that most of our passengers wear some type of hat or visor at some point on the cruise. We made an effort and actually think we may have spotted him about a half hour before the incident, but we did not get a good angle at his face." Jerry looked at the computer guy, who seemed to be one step ahead of us as the picture popped up on the monitor before Jerry said anything.

I picked him out of the mass of people without difficulty, but not because I recognized the face. Only about a third of his face was captured in the picture. The hat and the glasses stood out along with the shirt.

"No beard, mustache, but from this angle we can see a small mole or birthmark next to his ear. The picture is grainy because we've had to magnify the image," Jerry said.

"One thing we can say for sure, though," I said, "this person does not look like anyone from the wedding party and is definitely, well maybe not definitely, but certainly appears to be a man."

"We're not ready to give up on all the men in the wedding party, but we do agree with you that it seems highly unlikely that a woman is our killer," Jerry said. "Of course, anyone could be involved."

"That's true, but until we catch the killer, we're not going to have a chance at catching who else may be involved," Rose said.

Chapter 12

A little later, I sat with Rose at one of the few empty tables next to the pool and watched a man with a cast on his left leg walk out on deck on a pair of crutches.

"That would suck," I said.

"What?"

"To be on a cruise with a broken leg."

"You need to focus," Rose said. "If we're going to be any help at all, we need to come up with a plan."

"What plan," I asked. "We've got thousands of potential suspects, an unknown motive, and virtually no evidence. Any lab work that might give us a lead is days away, and everyone on this ship, other than the crew, will be long gone by then. Once we're ashore, they aren't going to let us tag along. They are only letting us help now because they are totally desperate."

"Think he'll strike again?"

I looked at her and thought about this for a moment. "It's possible."

"What kind of answer is that?"

"Who knows, this guy could be insane with no motive," I said and had a thought. "If he is insane with no connection to either of the victims, then we may never catch him. There doesn't need to be a link or a motive. That's why serial killers are so hard to catch. It would be a waste of time to go with that theory, so let's think that he has a motive. What would it be?"

"Could have a grudge against the cruise line," Rose said. She pulled out a small paper notepad and wrote something down.

"He could have a motive to kill one of the two and killed the second to throw the investigation off track," I said.

"Could he have a motive against both?"

"You mean like the crewman and Lassiter both did something to piss him off?"

"Yes, but that seems to lead us back to the guy being crazy, killing people because they make him mad," Rose said. "My bet is that one of the two was the original target. Without that, like you said, we have no way to get to the bottom of this."

"If you go one step further, we need to assume that Lassiter was the main target simply to give our effort any chance at all."

She nodded.

"Are we really committed to trying to solve this?" I asked.

"Yes, don't ask that anymore."

"Ok, then what would you do if this took place back home?"

We sat there for the next half hour and made a list of investigative steps we would recommend to Jerry and his team along with a few we could handle on our own. When we finished, Rose left to phone Jerry from one of the ship's phones, and I ordered us a third drink.

While she was gone, I began to wonder if one of the guys in the wedding party could have slipped away and killed Lassiter. It would be possible, I knew, because people always disappear to go to the restroom or to go to the bar and get a drink, and no one thinks anything of it. But what about the first murder? I couldn't see a connection to the wedding group. Of course, I knew there didn't need to be one, but if I accepted that there didn't need to be a connection then why did there need to be a connection between Lassiter and his murderer?

I shook my head and tried to think of something else. Our drinks arrived, and I looked to see if Rose had come back out onto the deck. I didn't see her, but I noticed a couple of the crew standing together not far from the doorway that Rose used. I looked around and saw another set of two crewmen standing near one of the bars by the pool. Another couple walked slowly together up one deck from the poolside. These weren't the officers of the ship in their dress uniforms, but the ones that wore white and carried out the worker bee stuff. I had not seen them standing around in pairs like this before.

"I'm not sure if we came up with much that he hadn't thought about already," Rose said when she returned.

"Don't sit down," I said and stood up. "Grab your drink and let's go for a walk."

"What's up?"

"Nothing big, I just want to check something out, and I bet that Jerry and his team didn't think of everything we came up with. How could they compete with the world's best deputy and her loyal sidekick?"

"Sidekick? That's good. Maybe that's how I should introduce you." She reached out and took my hand.

"I've been called worse."

"Probably by me," she said grinning. "Where are we going?"

"Nowhere, I just want to check something out." I pointed out the pairs of crewman seemingly standing around doing nothing.

We went up the stairs and looked up and down the deck on this level.

"Over there," Rose said.

"And down there," I said, as we discovered two more pairs of crew personnel.

"Security?" Rose asked.

"My guess is that they're observers, not that they won't react if they see something."

"To supplement the too few and inefficient security cameras?"

"Yep, but this ship has to be twenty, twenty five years old. Security cameras on cruise ships weren't a priority back then. In fact, I doubt if the wiring took the addition of future cameras into consideration."

"Most things these days are wireless," Rose said, "not that that helps us at all."

We strolled around the ship and saw several more sets of observers posted at different locations.

"My guess is that the crew knows about the murders. I wonder if the ship's passengers will be informed," I said.

"By the way, Jerry told me they have Sarah going through the entire list of passengers to see if she recognizes anyone. That's about three thousand names, talk about long shots."

"Guess it's one of those steps that have to be done."

She nodded. "I guess they should be able to break out a list of anyone who lives in the New York area. That might help."

"Someone they failed to invite to the wedding?" I said.

"Hopefully the killer had a better motive than that."

"I don't know. Do you remember that cheerleader mom who killed her daughter's main competition in making the varsity team?"

"That didn't really happen, did it?" she asked.

"I think it did. There are a lot of crazy people out there."

"You know, if they tell the passengers about the murders, they might have a mini panic on their hands, and if they don't, they could get quite the backlash if something else happens."

It took me a second to realize she answered the question I had asked a minute earlier. "I agree, and I wonder how long it will take to hit the news?"

"I'm amazed it hasn't already." Rose said.

"They may have gotten some commitment from Sarah."

"But, don't you think one of her friends here might also be associated in some way with the news company she's with?"

"I would think so," I said. "We didn't delve much into their lives when we talked to them."

"You didn't get much past the weather," she said and squeezed my hand.

I would have argued with her except I thought she might be right. I didn't remember anything of significance from my conversations with any of Sarah's friends.

Chapter 13

E d sat at his favorite outdoor bar again. He also noticed the pairs of crew personnel now posted at various spots throughout the ship. In fact, a man and a woman dressed in clean white work attire stood only twenty feet to his right.

He felt calm. No, it was more than calm, he thought, he was content. The server brought him a cold beer. Ed took a sip and smiled at his reflection in the mirror behind the bar. They had no idea who he was. He looked over at the two members of the crew standing together. He wanted to ask them for whom they were looking, but he already knew the answer.

A short woman with a scowl on her face approached the bar and sat on a nearby stool. She turned her head in his direction and said, "Bastard."

"Who me?"

She looked at him, a bit of confusion now appearing in her eyes. "Oh, no, sorry. Not you." She sucked on the straw that went with a drink she had in her hand. The gurgling sound of the drink being empty emanated from the plastic cup.

"Hey," she called to the bar tender. She repeated her call before the bar tender noticed her and came over. "Another vodka and seven." That was it, no please, no thank you.

The bartender took her cup, tossed it into the trash, and began making her another drink.

"Gerald is the bastard, not you," she said and forced a smile on her face.

"Who's Gerald?" he asked.

"My crappy boyfriend. He's not very nice."

"That's too bad."

The bartender brought her a new drink, and she studied the receipt.

"These drink packages are great," she said and sucked down a large gulp through the straw. She reached into the drink and brought out a cherry which she popped it into her mouth. "That bastard has spent the whole day in the casino and the cigar bar with his new buddies. What am I supposed to do?"

"He's not your husband?"

She almost spit out the new gulp she was working on. Covering her mouth with her hand, she coughed and swallowed. "Husband? Even I'm not that desperate."

He didn't know what to say. Women had never been his specialty. This woman could be attractive, if she put some effort into it. She wore a dark blue tee shirt that did nothing for her, and her white shorts looked like they had been worn for at least two days in a row. He couldn't fault the shape her hair was in here on a moving ship, but still he didn't think the way she wore it did anything for her. Plus, her dark roots gave away the fact that she died her hair blond.

She surprised him by moving to the stool next to him. "How about you, are you married?"

"No, a long time ago I was, but it didn't last."

"That's too bad, none of mine lasted either. I've always had a hard time staying with one man," her eyes looked deep into his.

Part of him wanted to back away, but he sensed something deep down. His new persona was trying to tell him something, or was it trying to come out? He struggled to control it, like it was something he could turn off at a whim. "It's not like that," the voice in his head told him. "Let me help."

Ed froze with the realization that something wasn't right. Earlier he had thought this whispering in his mind had been some sort of mental role playing or strategizing. But now, this sounded like an actual voice, like someone else was talking to him.

"What are you thinking of?" the woman asked.

"Oh, nothing," he said to respond to her question, but then more words came out. "I didn't mean to imply that you were desperate, but I certainly understand being lonely."

"No one likes to be lonely."

"A woman like you shouldn't ever have to be lonely," he said, or to be more exact, The Wind said.

She smiled and reached over and touched his hand and then left it barely an inch away from his.

"My name is Sofi, with an f."

"One of my favorite names." While the words came out of Ed's mouth, he felt like The Wind had spoken, and he had become the observer in this conversation. Rather than struggle with The Wind, Ed felt a tremble of excitement.

"Are you serious?" she asked.

"Yes. I guess it goes back to a girl in high school I had a crush on."

"Did she know?"

"No, I never had the nerve to tell her and have regretted it ever since," he said and brushed his hand gently against her hand. Ed wanted to laugh at the line of BS; he had never cared for a Sofi or Sophia in high school. However, not only did Ed not laugh, he found himself strangely excited over the direction this conversation was headed.

"Oh, that's sad," she said and moved her hand on top of his. "Maybe for today, I can be that Sofi for you."

"You're sweet," Ed said.

She sucked the last of her drink through the straw. "One more?" she asked.

"Sure, why not?" He motioned for the waiter to bring her another but turned down one for himself, saying he still had some beer left.

They stayed at the bar until she finished her drink. As expected, it didn't take long, and when she stood to leave, she staggered a little. He could see that she needed a little help walking, so he put his arm around her. She didn't resist, nor did he expect her to resist.

"Ooh, I'm cold," she said as a blast of wind funneled through the pool area.

He reached down and pulled a dry towel off the back of a chair they were walking by and wrapped it around her shoulders. He took off his ball cap and put it on her head. She cooed softly and leaned in tight against him. The hat was not the one he had worn when he killed Lassiter. That one was long gone. He had purchased this hat a few hours earlier in one of the ship's stores and didn't think he would be keeping it very long either.

A feeling of uneasiness came over Ed. Role playing, that was all, he thought. He only pretended to be this other person, The Wind. However, he couldn't shake that feeling that he had become an observer rather than being in control of his own actions. Despite the feeling, he allowed this other imaginary persona, The Wind, to lead the woman to his cabin. He looked around before stepping into the room and saw no one.

"You have a balcony!" Sofi exclaimed.

"Of course," he said.

She hurried out to it. "I wish I had a balcony."

"You do now. Consider this cabin yours, too."

She spun around and kissed him. They held each other tight until The Wind moved Ed's hands over her body.

Chapter 14

"More wine?" I asked. Our dinner choices had been difficult. I wanted both the duck and the steak as my main course. I knew I could have both, but I didn't want to look like one of those passengers who ordered too much food because it was free. Actually, I was one of those passengers, but in Rose's presence I felt a need to scale back my gluttony.

"Please," she said, holding her glass out.

I poured the red wine into her glass before refilling mine.

"The steak was good. You should get it again tomorrow," I said and reached out to the third plate on the table to cut a large piece of the duck and put it on my plate. I had resisted the temptation to order it, but Rose had easily observed my dilemma and ordered the extra plate for us to share. What a woman, I thought, and started to regret picking such a short cruise.

"I might," she said. "By the way, I forgot to mention, but when I talked to Jerry earlier on the phone, he said they have an individual they're looking at for the first murder but can't link the guy to the second."

"Doesn't have to be a link. The second murder could simply be to confuse everyone, but what's the connection?"

"He didn't elaborate much except to say it was another member of the crew, and that the two had gotten into a fight not too long ago."

"Think they'll hang the whole thing on him just to get rid of it?" I asked.

"I sure hope not," Rose said. "Jerry didn't go into detail, but if the person he's referring to has an alibi for the time of Lassiter's murder, then he's not our guy, and there's no way the two murders were done by different people. We're looking at the same weapon, or nearly the same, and same type of attack on both victims."

"You don't have to convince me. Since the two victims are so unrelated, I still think we have only two logical possibilities. First, we have a serial killer, or second, one was the original target and the other was to make the investigation more difficult."

"Well it has done that. There is a scary third option," Rose said.

"What's that?"

"We have a lot of older teenagers and young adults on this cruise. Gangs have initiation steps, and I have seen situations where to fully be accepted into the gang a new member has to kill someone. Usually it's a rival gang member or someone who has been an irritant to the gang, but I could envision something like this being within the realm of possibility."

"A gang on a cruise?"

"Maybe a wealthy, spoiled kids gang."

"Let's hope not," I said.

"Let's hope no one else gets murdered."

"I still think the gang theory, while certainly plausible, is the least likely scenario for what we have here."

"Me, too," Rose said. "Who would even know that Lassiter was going to be on this cruise? For him to be the real target, a person would have to come with him or follow him onto this ship."

"Didn't you say that they had Sarah go over the manifest to

see if she could identify someone?"

"Yes, and Matt or one of the guys that knew Lassiter the best was going to look through the list of passengers, too. But, you know, going through a list of a few thousand names is not a very efficient way to come up with a suspect."

"I know, and without a full forensic team to go over the crime scenes, we may be spinning our wheels. At least with all the people the captain has out to watch what's going on, like those two over there, it will be hard for the killer to get to someone else." I pointed to two crew personnel walking outside the window by our table. "I bet he'll have them out watching twenty four hours a day."

"Unless the killer is totally insane, I can't imagine why he or she would want to risk another murder on the ship," Rose said.

"Well, he's got to be insane since he's killed two people already; normal people don't do that. But, if we're trying to apply logic to this, I agree with you. Why risk getting caught by committing another murder?"

"You know, we're doing just what an old mentor of mine told me to never do. He said for me not to try to figure out a killer by imagining what I would do next. We're not killers, so we don't think like killers."

"Okay."

"He said it's appropriate to try to guess ahead and make a list of possibilities, but not to put too much weight on what you would do if you were in her shoes."

"Makes sense to me," I said. "I've never understood why anyone would want to kill anyone else, other than in self defense or to protect another person. Now, I could see shooting someone in the knee simply to punish them."

That brought a grin to Rose's face. "Don't think I haven't thought of that before, although I was thinking of another part of the man's anatomy at the time."

"I hope no one we know."

"Not you, silly, this guy was a pervert abusing kids. My partner and I stumbled upon him and this little boy parked in a car out of town. When my partner went to call it in, the creep got out of the car, and I had the perfect opportunity to neuter him. I almost did, too."

"Who would blame you?"

"I know, and I still think my desire to do so at the time was normal. What the guy on this ship is doing is premeditated murder, and while he may have had a grievance against one of the two, I can't imagine he could have a legitimate grievance against both."

"That just takes us back to square one," I said.

"Excuse me, I was asked to bring this to you," the maître d stood there with a small white envelope in his hand. "For you," he said and offered the envelope to Rose. She took it, and he walked away.

She showed the front of the envelope to me, and I saw that it had been addressed to Deputy Luna.

"From Jerry?" I asked.

She opened it and nodded. "He wants us to come see him after we finish eating."

Chapter 15

The meeting with Jerry didn't amount to much. They had nothing new to tell us concerning the investigation, and it seemed to me that the cruise line had already decided to push the investigation off the ship as soon as we docked in Galveston.

"Deputy Luna," Jerry said, using her official title. "In a little over forty-eight hours we'll be docking in Galveston, and all the passengers will be disembarking. A small percentage of the crew will also be leaving the ship. The decision has been made to brief the FBI, US Customs, and the Texas Attorney General on the fact that two murders have been committed onboard and that the killer could possibly be among the people disembarking in Galveston."

"Ok," Rose said.

"Included in the brief that we will be providing, will be the fact that we've made you aware of our investigation. We will suggest that since we'll be going back out to sea with the ship on the same day that we arrive, that they take advantage of your knowledge, Deputy, if they decide to pursue their own investigation into the matter. We do not intend to make any mention of you, Jim."

"I don't mind, but how could any US court have jurisdiction over this, even if we identify a suspect?" Rose said.

"It's complicated, and I'm not a lawyer, but if we don't catch the man before we dock, we have no other choice. We can't keep everyone on the ship. Our investigation will go on, as there is always the possibility that the killer is one of us, but we have an obligation to advise the American authorities. They may choose to do nothing to investigate the matter, but that is out of our hands."

I didn't say anything, but my bet was on his last sentence. The various agencies would keep a record of whatever the cruise line passed on to them, but that was about it. How could they do anything?

"What about the bodies?" Rose asked.

"That is still under discussion. We have done enough to substantiate death and means of death, but extensive forensic medical examinations are required. A decision will be made before we reach Galveston on what to do with Mr. Lassiter's body. Don't take me wrong, it will be returned to his widow, but whether or not we transport the body elsewhere for medical examination is still being debated."

"It would seem a lot more efficient to let it be done in Galveston," I said.

"I agree, and I believe that will be the decision that is made," Jerry said.

"If you identify a suspect before we dock, and it's not a ship's employee, what can the ship's captain do?" Rose asked.

"A captain of a ship has tremendous power over what goes on aboard his ship. That includes disciplining someone for breaking the law. We don't have a plank that we can make someone walk, and keel hauling has not been used as a punishment for well over a hundred years, at least to my knowledge," he smiled at the thought. "We have a brig, and we do have procedures to adjudicate matters like this. We have to have these processes as crimes committed at sea are beyond the jurisdiction of any nation."

"Your ship flies under the Bahamian flag. Couldn't they do something?" I asked.

"We have arrangements with them to transfer prisoners to their jails, if that is what you mean. The cruise line can also argue civil cases through their courts, I believe. However, what is most important is the fact that out at sea, we follow maritime law, and under that the captain is king."

Rose looked at me like she had a question.

"Don't look at me for further elaboration. I was in the air force not the navy. I know in the air force the pilot is in charge of the plane, but that's a lot different from being a captain of a ship, I think."

Jerry grinned at us. "Rose, I appreciate your willingness to help. Yours, too, Jim. We haven't given up yet, but to be honest, our main focus at this point is to not let another incident occur. Feel free to ask me anything before we dock, and I promise you we will keep you informed if we develop anything of substance."

"Do you still have reinforcements arriving to help out with the investigation?" I asked.

"No, at least not yet. Wiser minds than mine decided that oversight and investigative guidance could be provided through video conferencing."

I thought I could detect a little disappointment in his voice, and I couldn't blame him. While online guidance was better than nothing, it woefully lacked the effectiveness of experienced eyes at the scene.

"Will you be sharing photos of the crime scenes?" Rose asked.

"Yes, virtually everything."

"Does Sarah Lassiter know what you'll be doing with her

husband's body?"

"Not yet, but we have not kept it from her. She has not asked us, and I would prefer to know myself before I told her."

It struck me odd that Sarah hadn't asked.

"Have you informed his family?" I asked.

"We informed his wife. It is her responsibility to inform other members of his family," Jerry said.

"When you get a response back from the U.S. authorities, will you provide me with whatever contact information they share with you?" Rose asked.

"Of course, but I don't have anything yet."

We left Jerry a few minutes later, and while we were walking through the lobby area, Rose suddenly stopped. "Let's go talk to Sarah."

"Ok, but we don't have much to tell her," I said.

"I know. We haven't done anything," Rose said, and I sensed disappointment in her voice.

I wanted to say that she had known this was going to be an impossible task from the beginning, but I knew that comment wasn't what she needed to hear.

"Think she's in her cabin?" I asked.

"Yes."

A different crewman guarded her door, and we had to go through the procedure of telling him who we were and for him to check with Sarah to see if we were welcome. The routine only caused a slight delay.

She had not changed clothes since we saw her in the morning. A tray with half eaten food was on the dresser. A wine bottle had been open, but it looked three quarters full.

"Have you learned anything?" she asked after she hugged us

both. Her bloodshot eyes and uncombed hair supported my belief that she had spent the whole day in her room.

"Not really, but we have a lot to tell you, and a lot to ask you. Are you going to be okay with that?" I asked.

"Sure," she said and sat down on her bed.

Rose and I sat down next to each other on the small couch.

"Want to tell her what we've learned from Jerry?" I asked Rose.

She nodded and proceeded to give Sarah a very thorough briefing on everything we had learned that day.

"So were they random murders?" she asked.

"Could be, but one of the two could have been targeted, and the other murder done to confuse everything," Rose said.

I watched Sarah scratch the back of her left hand. She seemed to be doing it without thinking, and I could see that she had created a reddish area that looked like it could start bleeding any moment. The hand had looked normal in the morning.

"Why would someone be doing this?" she asked.

"We don't know. Do you have any questions for us?" Rose asked.

"No. I can't get past the 'who and why' questions in my head, although I've also begun asking the 'why me' question which I know is selfish."

"You do understand Joe's body might not be available right after the cruise," I said.

"That's okay, it'll give me time to talk to his family and figure out what to do. I never thought about this happening."

"That's understandable," I said.

"Sarah, when you went through the passenger list, did any of the names stand out to you?" Rose asked.

"No, but there were so many names I kept thinking some of the names might be from my childhood like Beverly Williams and Suzanne Kassler. Those are names of friends I had like in the sixth grade. They also showed me a shortened list of names from the New York area, but that didn't help. They were supposed to have Matt go over the list, too. He knew Joe better than anyone, even me."

"Has he talked to you about any of the names?" I asked.

"No, I haven't seen him other than right after we learned of … it happening." She paused before finishing the sentence as though she was searching for a way to end the sentence without saying Joe's death or Joe's murder.

"The ship's security team is running a number of computer searches to try to identify closer links between any of the passengers and Joe, but these are long shots. They have a security camera shot of someone they believe to be the murderer. We've convinced them that they should show that video to you and the rest of the wedding party to see if anyone can recognize him," I said.

"Then they must know who he is," Sarah said. "Why haven't they showed it to us already?"

"Because they had to be sure no one from your group was involved. They still have their suspicions, but it's become fairly obvious that none of you were directly involved," Rose said.

"Directly," Sarah said in a voice a little more agitated.

"It's just something they have to consider," I said.

"Can't they identify the person in the video?"

"No, they don't have a good look at his face," I said.

"There are all types of very good facial recognition software out there today," Sarah said.

"They are in the process of trying to get some right now, but as you can imagine this is a cruise ship with no expertise in all this. They sent copies to their corporate office, and more stuff is being done there, too. Our biggest problem is that in a couple of days, our killer may be leaving the ship," I said.

"The guy has committed the perfect murder," Sarah said.

"No. There's no such thing," Rose said.

"Have you notified your office?" I asked.

"No. I feel sick and a little guilty over all this," she said. "I know the Sarah you knew was all business, the story meant more than anything, but this is hard. I can see a story there, but every time I think of telling it, it makes me sick."

"We're not encouraging you to contact them. It was just a question we had to ask," I said. "Has anyone else been around to see you since we were here earlier today?"

"Everyone, and I had to go down and review the passenger list. I wish I could disappear. I know I'm ruining everyone's cruise."

"Sarah, that's silly. You haven't done anything to cause any of this," Rose said.

"I know, but I have messed up your cruise. You don't need to waste any more time on it. I should never have asked you. It's impossible." A tear leaked out of her left eye and trailed down by her nose.

"Don't worry about us," Rose said. "You need to try to get some rest. Tomorrow we may get a break or two."

"I'm not tired, but I do need to make a list of things I need to do when we dock. I guess some of the things I should do tomorrow." Sarah didn't elaborate, and we didn't ask.

Chapter 16

When Ed woke the next morning, he did so with a start. He looked around in the cabin and saw that everything looked normal. He relaxed and wondered for a moment if everything had been a dream. He had almost convinced himself it was, but then he saw strands of the woman's hair on the pillow next to him.

How long had he been out of control? He thought he had pretended to be someone else when he killed Joe Lassiter, and maybe there was a small moment of pretense when he killed the young crewman, but yesterday and last night? Had it been almost sixteen hours? How could that be possible?

"Relax," a voice in his head told him. "You know you enjoyed every minute of it."

"Be quiet," he said out loud. A bead of sweat formed on his forehead. He climbed out of bed, feeling a twinge of pain in his lower back and hurried to the shower. He had to figure this out, and he had to get rid of the feeling that his body was covered with her sweat, her scent, her DNA. "What did you do?" he shouted.

"You loved every minute of it," The Wind whispered in his mind.

"No, not all, it was not in the plan."

He stood still while the hot water poured over him. Not all, he thought again, not the end. How did he let that happen? He would have to reassert himself now and push this creation of his,

The Wind, back into the recesses of his mind and lock it away there forever. He could do it, he told himself. He was not crazy.

Sex. That was all it was supposed to be about. He was uncomfortable with the woman. He had never been comfortable around women, especially when they got loud and aggressive. He considered getting up and walking away from the bar when this other, inner persona who had somehow gotten into his mind wanted a chance with her. Role playing he had told himself. He had given into the idea, but he thought he still had control.

The rest of the day and into the evening he had been content to be an observer. No, he was more than that. He lived, felt, and enjoyed every moment of the day, but he had not been in charge of his own behavior. How could that be, he wondered.

The day had been exhilarating. No, it had been more than that. He had never been like that with a woman, and she was more than a willing participant. She had actually led him, pushed him to do things, and she appeared to enjoy the day as much as he had. Some of the things they did, things that she had initiated, now made him feel uncomfortable and thinking about them, a little dirty.

To be fair, she had a lot to drink before they left the bar and even more after they returned to his cabin. He had taken advantage of that, and he had never taken advantage of a drunken woman before. But that he could excuse. Being aware that the amount of alcohol flowing through her might play to their advantage when they left the bar did not mean he forced her to drink or do anything.

"Their advantage?" he said out loud. Why would he think that? "It was only me. There are not two of us!" Despite the tone of his voice, he sensed laughter coming from somewhere deep inside his mind.

He turned the water to cold and forced himself to focus.

Everything had been fun and games, he thought. No damage done until the end. He turned off the water and closed his eyes. He wanted to change what happened but knew he couldn't.

Ed could remember waking up in the night, but in his mind the vision of what occurred after that seemed less clear than his recall of what happened before they fell asleep. The clock said it was a few minutes after one, and Sofi slept next to him, snoring softly. For some reason that he could not now imagine, he got out of bed and grabbed a belt from the top drawer of his dresser. He returned to the bed and without a second thought wrapped the belt around her throat and strangled her. She struggled, but he kept his knee on her back and put his weight onto that knee while he pulled up and tightened the belt. Once she was unconscious, he didn't even know if she was dead, he picked her up and tossed her over the balcony. That must be what caused his back to be stiff this morning, but why did he do it? Why?

He could feel her body in his hands as he lifted her over the rail on the balcony, but why did he do it? The more he thought about it, the more it confused him, the more it angered him, and the more it scared him.

"You wanted a third body," the voice in his mind said. "It was in your plan."

"Not that way, not her," he said aloud. "Sofi was mixed up, but she was nice, and I liked her. Why did you have to kill her?"

"You?" The Wind whispered. "Don't you mean we?"

"No, there's only me!" he shouted. "You don't exist." He began to cry. "Focus!" he yelled at himself.

There had to be ways he could get rid of this other persona.

He would do some research. He was good at research, and the internet had to have a lot of information on what he was going through. This thought calmed him a little.

First, though, he had to clean up his room. He removed the sheets and pillow cases and piled them on the floor. He grabbed a wash cloth from the bathroom, and after getting it damp, he started to wipe off every surface area he could find in the room. At least he didn't see blood anywhere.

He looked around the room and looked for Sofi's clothing. Not seeing any, he wondered what happened to them. His memory of last night ended as he watched Sofi's body tumble into the dark, night air. Why was that? He had to have gone back into the room and back to bed. Had he lost total awareness? He concentrated, and after a few seconds, he remembered gathering up all her clothing, bundling them tightly together along with his shoes, and throwing everything into the water below. This memory felt more like a vision. He could not remember touching the clothing, and why his shoes?

"They were evidence. We couldn't let anyone discover the blades hidden in them, and we won't need them anymore," The Wind whispered.

A chill went through the man. He did not remember making a decision to throw away the shoes. It did not matter to him that the shoes were gone, but the fact that he could now see himself tossing the clothing and shoes overboard without any memory as to why he did so confirmed the realization that he had lost control of his own actions. He could not let that happen again.

After inspecting the room for a third time, he finished dressing and left his cabin nearly knocking over the young Asian man who served as his cabin steward.

"Excuse me," he said. "Could I have new sheets today?"

"Certainly," the young man said and smiled. "You party here last night."

"Not all night," Ed said and hurried away. My God, he thought, what does the steward know? How can he explain Sofi's presence in his room? Would they know if she left or not? He stopped walking and looked up and down the hallway. He didn't see any security cameras, but to be sure, he retraced his steps, walked by his room, and kept walking until he reached the aft elevators. He didn't see any cameras.

Somewhat relieved, he continued on to the dining room where he noticed security cameras both outside the dining room and inside. As the hostess was taking him to a table, he had a thought.

"Excuse me, I need to go get something. I'll be right back," he said. Rather than return to his room, he went directly to the outdoor bar area where he met Sofi and studied the surroundings for cameras. He located two. Neither one was aimed at the bar, but both would have captured his departure from the area with Sofi. He felt a cold sweat begin to run down his chest. He had been so careful, he thought, and now this.

Should he turn himself in and plea for help? Could he be insane? He discarded the idea, he would first fight to get rid of this other creature trying to control his mind.

Chapter 17

"I know why you prefer eating here rather than the dining room," Rose said, after I returned to the table with more bacon.

"My plate is giving me away?"

"Blaming it on the plate doesn't cut it. How much weight do you think we have gained on this cruise already?"

"Oh, I don't know. You don't look like you have gained anything," I said.

"Ha!"

"And I plan on going on a strict diet when I get back home," I lied.

"We may have to do some laps today," Rose said and removed the last cinnamon roll from my plate, putting it on hers.

"I'll get my exercise from going back and forth to the food counters." I stood and walked off toward the nearby stack of pastry. Luck was with me as a new tray of cinnamon rolls arrived at the counter a second before me.

After putting two rolls on my plate, I started back to our table when I bumped into Jerry. He had a picture of a woman in his hand and had been scouring the passengers around him.

"Pardon me. Oh it's you," he said.

"What's up?"

He looked more serious and more stressed than before. In fact, in our earlier meetings he looked well in control despite having two murders tossed on his plate. He showed me the picture.

"Do you know this woman?"

"No, I don't recognize her at all. Bring it over to Rose, maybe she knows her." I pointed to our table.

He started off without waiting for me. "Deputy Luna, do you recognize this woman?"

Rose took the picture and looked at it. "No. Is this related?"

"God, I hope not. She's been missing since yesterday afternoon. Usually, we would wait her disappearance out for twenty-four hours. Shipboard romances pop up all the time, but with what's going on, I have a terrible feeling in my gut."

"I bet it's nothing," Rose said.

"Let's hope you're correct. Her friend said she was supposed to meet him for dinner, but didn't. They share a cabin, and he claimed she never returned last night. When she didn't show up for an eight o'clock spa appointment this morning, he came to us. He's convinced something has happened to her."

"You have people out looking for her?" I said, noticing another member of the crew walking around with a picture in his hand.

"Yes, and a page for her earlier this morning went unanswered."

"The other victims were not hidden. He left them where he killed them. Shouldn't someone have found the body by now?" I said.

He sat down at our table and motioned for a nearby crewman working the dining area to bring him some coffee. I offered him one of the cinnamon rolls.

"This is terrible. The thought that she may be a prisoner being kept alive for whatever purpose before being killed sickens me. We're frigging powerless."

"Can't your stewards inspect every room on the ship," Rose asked.

"Yes, and we're in the process of implementing that right now, but rushing something like this creates a public relations nightmare. About twenty percent of our passengers don't want to be disturbed in their cabins before lunch. We're going to run a short notice safety exercise, repeating the one we did before we departed."

"You mean where everyone has to report out on deck at their designated assembly areas?" I asked.

"Yes, but we won't do it until eleven. By then we hope to find her, so we won't have to do it at all."

"How are the captain and crew holding up?" I asked.

"Not well. There's already talk among the crew that the ship is cursed. I've gotten some informal feedback from the home office that there will be a board of inquiry and key personnel changes may be necessary, but that's not important right now. We've got to find this woman and catch our murderer."

"Has Mrs. Lassiter been around to see the video of the suspect yet?" Rose asked.

"I don't know. My technician is handling that alone this morning. Everyone else is busy. I feel like we're being manipulated. We should be putting all our effort into identifying the killer, but instead, we are looking for this woman."

"If the disappearance is related, then I think our killer is pulling the strings. However, he'll make a mistake if he keeps this up," I said.

"Keeps this up? Don't even think that," Jerry said and bit into the cinnamon roll.

I looked at Rose, but neither of us said anything.

"I think we've eliminated most of the crew," Jerry said. "We cannot be positive, of course, but between the security video and the time of the incidents, we're fairly certain the murderer is not a member of the crew."

"Then you have made some progress, one thousand down and three thousand to go," I said.

"Thanks," Jerry said, and Rose shot me a look.

"You know if I came on board intent on killing Lassiter, it might make sense to kill someone else to throw the investigation off track, but it would be a serious risk, and I'd have to be very cold hearted," I said.

"How does that help us?" Rose said.

"It doesn't except once I killed my main target, why go after someone else?"

"Playing the devil's advocate," Rose said, "why not make it three to throw everything into a frenzy? Besides, maybe the killer only planned to kill two people, and this woman came along and fell into his lap as a victim of opportunity. He simply took advantage of it."

"One thing we'd be doing if we were back stateside is going to Lassiter's friends, family, and co-workers and interviewing them. They might recognize someone on the passenger list," I said.

"We will be sharing everything with the U.S. authorities soon, later today I think. Unfortunately, the corporate office's first reaction is always to prevent bad publicity," Jerry said.

"Well, in their defense, if the NYPD gets a list of three thousand names to run through for a crime committed outside their jurisdiction, it wouldn't be put on the fast track," I said.

"The more I think about it, the more I think we're dealing with a very smart person, and that's not good for us," Rose said.

"Thanks, you two are making my day even better. I ought to get back to work." He said he would see us later and walked off.

"I guess we didn't cheer him up," I said.

"I wouldn't be surprised if he loses his job after this cruise."

"Me either."

"The captain, too," she added.

"Do you think this woman is connected?" I asked.

"If they don't find her, then yes."

"A victim of opportunity?"

"Yes, I can't imagine a person could come on board planning to kill three people on a five-day cruise. Even two is a stretch."

"What was that your mentor once told you about putting yourself in the killer's shoes?" I asked.

"Touche'. Why would the killer think like me?"

"I don't know what would be worse, finding her and linking her death to the killer, or she never shows up, and no one ever knows what happened to her," I said.

"You mean like if she fell overboard or committed suicide by jumping overboard."

"Exactly. Either way she's dead, but if her death is deemed independent of the killer, then I think the fallout on the ship's leadership may be more severe."

"Depending on the press they get, I wouldn't be surprised if they rename the ship," Rose said.

I doubted that they would go that far and was about to express my doubts, when I remembered a friend of mine in the air force. He commanded a flying wing, and from everything I saw was doing a great job. Two aircraft accidents occurred under his watch, and shortly after the second one he was relieved of his command. I remembered his stoic acceptance of his firing. He even made the comment that the "buck stops here." Despite his acceptance of the whole thing, it did make me wonder who decided where the buck should stop. Maybe the person one step above him?

"Here comes the wedding party," Rose said. "Well, most of them anyway." We watched as they made their way to one of the food lines. They didn't appear to see us.

"To be honest, I would just as soon avoid them," I said.

"Because we haven't done anything to solve Joe's murder?"

"No, and that's not true. We've given advice and feedback to Jerry and his folks. You know, it's not like you and I can start calling in passengers to interview."

"I know, and I didn't mean it that way. It's frustrating."

"Amen," I said.

Chapter 18

Rose and I strolled around the ship for a while before returning to our cabin. Shortly after entering the room, Rose noticed the message light flashing on the phone. She picked up the receiver and listened to the message.

"They got a break," she said as she put the receiver down. "Jerry wants us to come down to his office."

"That was quick. We just saw him. Did the message say what it was?"

"No. Maybe they found the woman."

We left our cabin and headed down to meet Jerry. He was waiting for us, and we followed him back into the complex of offices.

"We've got your friend Matt in there," Jerry motioned to the room where they had interviewed me.

"You think he's involved?" Rose asked.

"Could be, he claimed not to recognize any of the names of the roster, and then later yesterday, he's at the Seaside Lounge with two of them."

"He lied to you," I said.

"Yes, and he's admitted to that. He claims he's known the two for a long time and even knew they would be onboard. He just didn't want to get them involved, since, get this, he knows they wouldn't kill anybody and says they didn't even know Lassiter."

"Stupid," I said.

"While we can exclude Matt personally from the killings, we

can't exclude his friends. One of them is even the same size and shape as our man in the video."

"What have they told you?" Rose asked.

"We just pulled the two men in. So far they are playing dumb and are acting indignant. One of them has already threatened to sue us," Jerry said. "They claimed they didn't know about Lassiter's murder which was stupid, since Matt readily admitted to discussing it with the two."

"How did you put the three together?" Rose asked.

"It's easy to trace the activities of someone on the ship if they use their sea card. We've been monitoring Matt's activities since we discovered Lassiter murdered. We flagged the passengers from the New York area late yesterday."

I imagined Rose and I were being monitored, too. "Now, their lying to you about not knowing about Lassiter's murder doesn't help either. Have you gone back to Sarah and asked her if she knows the two?" I asked.

"She's already said she didn't know the names," he said.

"Like Matt?" I asked.

He only grinned.

"What can we do to help?"

"We have the ability to conduct name checks, limited background checks, and such, but none of them are very thorough. More importantly, nothing we can do is quick. Rose, you could do these in a fraction of the time. If we give you these two guys info, would you check them for us?"

"I'd have to use my laptop, but with the ship's Wi-Fi, I should be able to do it. Have you passed my name to the federal and state agencies?"

"That brief should have gone out last night. The copy we

received to coordinate on did have your name on it. I don't know what reaction the brief may have received or if any correspondence was sent back in return," Jerry said.

"Good, that will help if I get any resistance," Rose said.

"Resistance?" Jerry asked.

"From my sheriff, it's personal, nothing that should concern you."

A knock at the door interrupted us. The door opened and I recognized Johann Needles, the ship's officer who had interviewed me earlier. He stuck his head in, "Jerry, I need to see you for a second."

Jerry got up and left the room.

"Think they found her?" I asked.

"I hope she's okay."

"If they haven't, and this is something else, maybe we should talk to the guy who came with her on the cruise. Could be he wanted to kill her all along, and the other two were just to throw everyone off the track."

"He'd have to be awful stupid and sick to do it this way," I said. "The guy who's doing this doesn't impress me as being stupid."

"Would it be the first time you were wrong?"

I had to smile. More than once we had talked about how someone we thought to be guilty or innocent in the middle of an investigation had turned out the opposite in the end.

Jerry walked back in the room. "It's hit the news. Not widespread, but it will be soon, I'm sure. We will not be stopping today at Progresso, and instead will be heading straight back to Galveston."

"I can't imagine how the passengers will react," Rose said.

"We've already taken extra security measures and will further enhance them. The captain will be running a ten minute presentation that will be run repeatedly on the ship's televisions. There will also be a letter placed in every stateroom later today. I hope their reaction isn't too extreme."

"No sign of the missing woman yet?" Rose asked.

"No, and it's getting to the point that we believe she's no longer on the ship. I need to do a few things. Deputy, can I get you to run the names now?"

"Sure. Give me the details, and I'll go do it right now."

When we reached the door leaving the inner offices, we ran into most of the wedding party being escorted back in. We got looks that implied to me that we were now considered traitors. Sheila, in particular, gave me a stern look. Only Jill, Sarah's cousin, grabbed my arm and asked what was happening.

"Just some follow up," I said.

"Come along," one of their security escorts said.

Jill let go of my arm and gave me a half smile before chasing after the group.

"No Sarah," I said.

"She may already be here. Looks like her friends might be blaming us for their being called back for questioning. I hope that's not going to put you in a spot with Sarah."

"They'll figure it out pretty quick. Matt caused his own problem, and in doing so, he cast more suspicion on all of them. Besides, I don't care if they want to blame us," I said.

"We forgot to ask Jerry for the name of the boyfriend of the missing woman," Rose said. "I'd like to run his name through the system, too. Wait for me here, I'll be right back." She disappeared through the doorway.

I leaned against a display counter and grabbed a pamphlet about cruises through the Panama Canal.

"I understand you are helping in the investigation."

Looking up, I saw Inga standing a few feet away.

"Doing what we can," I said. "How do you keep your uniform so well pressed?"

"We don't have a choice, and the ship's cleaners do all the work. I just wear them."

And wear them well, I thought. "How are you doing with all this going on? Must be hectic and stressful for everyone."

"It's not good," she said. "I don't know why this is happening. We've never had anything like this happen before."

"I hope not. Two murders and now a missing woman, I imagine it's a record for bad things to happen on a cruise, other than the ship sinking."

"Don't even think that. There are already rumors going around among the crew that someone has a bomb on board."

"Let's hope that is only a rumor," I said.

"I hope you can help us catch him," she said. "We need to stop him, and I think when we do, we should throw him overboard."

"Walk the plank?"

She smiled, "Yes! Please catch him, Jim." She surprised me by reaching out with both hands and squeezed my right hand.

Rose came out the door, and if by some natural instinct, Inga turned and walked away.

"Am I breaking something up? Rose asked.

"No, she knows we're helping out and wants us to solve this thing quickly."

"Beautiful, isn't she?"

"Oh no, she's too tall for me," I said.

"Liar," she said and poked my side with her finger. "Let's head back to the room. I can run these names, and you can take a cold shower."

"You go do that. I want to walk a couple laps around the ship and think. I'll be up in thirty to forty minutes."

Once outside on the fifth deck, I walked to the location where the first murder took place. Two crewmen stood by an area cordoned off, maybe fifteen feet by fifteen feet. They didn't pay much attention to me as I stopped and studied the area. I could see that two of the steel plates had been recently painted. I knew that the man killed had been stripping and repainting the plates. In addition to the cordon, a makeshift canvas lean-to had been set up against the railing next to the steel plates. Its most likely purpose was to conceal the actual scene until someone could give it a more thorough scrutiny; however, standing off to the side, a person could see under the canvas.

I thought I could see blood stains on the deck under the lean-to, but walking around I didn't see any other signs of blood on the deck. I wondered if the killer walked up to him in the dark or had been waiting here for him to arrive. There wasn't a good hiding spot nearby; however, I imagined at night someone could stand against the wall and be hard to see.

I left the scene of the first murder and walked to the scene of the second. Like at the first, two crewmen stood outside an area that had been cordoned off. Another canvas lean-to stretched from the outside wall of the ship to the deck where it was held in place by several paint cans. I wondered how effective the canvas cover would be in protecting the scene.

Remembering the video I watched, I retraced the steps I believed the killer took leaving the scene. A waste of time, I thought, since I didn't see anything. A strong wind, partly caused by the ship's movement through the sea, blew in my face. Despite the lean-to, the wind had undoubtedly blown a lot of extraneous debris into the crime scene thereby compromising it. I didn't know who the cruise line was sending in to do a more in-depth forensic examination, but I figured by now it, too, would be a waste of time.

Two more crewmen leaned against the railing about a hundred yards from the spot where Lassiter died. Yesterday, I had thought that the presence of so many of the crew personnel standing around and being so obvious would prevent the killer from striking again. Now, I wondered if it simply caused him to change tactics.

In the distance, I saw a helicopter. I didn't give it a second thought until I noticed it was approaching the ship. Returning inside, I took the elevator up to the pool deck. By the pool, I realized I still needed to go up one more level to get a good view of the helicopter. It seemed like a dozen or so other passengers had the same idea making me fall to the back of the line of people climbing the poolside stairs. For some reason they bunched up at the top of the stairs, and I had to push my way through. As I did, I brushed by a man.

"Excuse me," I said.

He glared at me, but didn't say anything. I walked by him but had a strange feeling. I stopped, turned, and looked at him. He stared back. Instinctively, I turned away and walked over to a spot against the railing where I had a good view of the helicopter. My mind, however, kept thinking about the man. Was he the one in the video? I glanced back and saw him going down the stairs. I followed him.

Chapter 19

"Hey, wait up," I said.

The man stopped and turned around. Nothing in his eyes or posture seemed friendly. I stopped a few feet from him giving him some space. "What's your name? I mean, you look familiar. Were you ever in the air force?"

"You don't know me," he said but didn't move.

"Come on, I'm Jim West." I offered my hand.

He ignored it. "What's going on?"

"Nothing. Maybe it's not you, but do you have a brother that looks like you? I know I've seen you before. I just can't remember where."

"Where are you from?" he asked, thawing a little.

"All over, I must have lived in ten different locations with the air force. That's what makes it hard to place someone."

"Well, if you were never in the New York area you wouldn't have seen me or my brother." He turned and walked away.

I returned to the stairs, but I kept an eye on the man. He went to the bar by the pool and ordered something. I went on up the stairs but kept watching him. After the bartender gave him a beer, he walked away. I waited a minute or two and went down to the same bar.

"Can I talk to you for a second," I asked the bartender.

"A drink?" he asked. His name tag indicated he was from Malaysia and listed his name as Johnny.

"Not at the moment, Johnny. I'm helping Jerry Bergren in the investigation of the missing woman and the two murders." He took a step back. "You can check. My name is Jim West. I need to know the name of the man that was here a minute ago and bought the beer from you."

After a moment of hesitation, he went back to his register and pushed a few buttons. He returned with a copy of the receipt. I studied the receipt, seeing the name Stinson, and looked up at Johnny to thank him. He stared past me with surprise or fear in his eyes. I turned, and Stinson grabbed the front of my shirt and slammed me back against the counter.

"Get what you want, asshole?" he said.

"I only -" I didn't get to say more as he cut me off.

"If I see you around me at anytime on this cruise, I will mess up that pretty face of yours. Got it?"

I forced myself to relax, despite the urge to rip his hand off my shirt. "Yes, I just wanted to know."

He gave me a slight push, let go, and walked away.

"Are you okay?" Johnny asked.

Another waiter had come alongside him.

"Yes, I'm fine, and thanks for getting me his name."

"Is he the one?" Johnny asked.

"I don't know, but that's what we are trying to find out."

"He's not a nice guy."

I grinned. "That's for sure."

Before heading back to my cabin, I hustled to a spot where I could see the helicopter. It landed before I had a view of it, but I did get to see three men with heavy looking metal cases get off and walk across the deck to meet the captain. The experts, I thought, better late than never.

By the time I got to the cabin, Rose had finished making the query on the computer and sat on the balcony with a cup of coffee in her hand.

"Sorry, this was the last pack," she said, referring to the coffee.

"That's alright. I have another name for you to trace." I held up the receipt.

"Who's that?"

"Only have a last name and a cabin number right now, but I'll get the rest. I saw him up by the pool. He looks like the guy in the video."

"We didn't get a very good look at his face."

"I know, but this guy really overreacted when I approached him. He's not very nice and definitely didn't want to tell me his name."

She looked at me like she was thinking "that's it?"

"I know it's not much to go on, but I just had this feeling," I said. "Did you see the helicopter?"

"No, what helicopter?"

"One just arrived and dropped off three men who I believe are forensic or investigative experts. Despite Jerry last saying no one was coming to help, they're here. They were carrying those big silver cases." I didn't have to elaborate, as Rose knew to what I was referring. All law enforcement agencies of any size have similar forensic or crime scene kits that they carry around in silver or black cases unless they're fortunate enough to have a dedicated van they can drive to crime scenes. Obviously, driving a van out here was not an option.

"Think it'll do any good?" she asked.

"I doubt it, but I wonder how it will affect us."

"Very little, since they've already committed to having me be their interface with whatever U.S. agencies want to get involved."

"I've been thinking about that, too, and the more I do, the more I think no American agency is going to get involved. These crimes happened out at sea and from their point of view, without us handing over an American suspect to them, they're going to think that there is about as good a chance that the murderer is a non-U.S. citizen who stayed on the boat when it left. One of the victims was not an American, and the missing woman may have accidently fallen overboard or committed suicide. What would your sheriff say?"

"He wouldn't touch it. We've got more work than we can handle, and I imagine that's the same most everywhere else."

"My point exactly, we've got less than two days to solve this, or it will never get resolved. Maybe we ought to keep our fingers crossed that these experts can turn the tide," I said.

"Well, go get the rest of your suspect's ID, and I'll send out another trace."

I didn't have to go far. Using the room phone I called Jerry's office, and in less than ten seconds, one of his staff provided me all the information I needed. The man's name was Gerald E. Stinson. Along with his name, I now also had his date of birth and his passport number.

"Here's his info," I said and handed Rose the note pad I used. "Can you get his social security number by cross checking his passport number?"

"With this handwriting, you should have been a doctor."

"Come on, it's not that bad."

She grinned at me. "Yes, I can work with this." She got up and went inside.

I sat down in her chair, stretched my legs, and seeing that she left her coffee, I took a sip. Too sweet, so I left the rest for her. I closed my eyes and let the fresh air help me relax.

"Guess what?" she said a few minutes later.

I opened my eyes and looked up at her. "What?"

"Not much of a guess, but the only hit I got was on your boy Stinson. He's got quite the record. Looks like he may have connections to, if I can use an old term, the mob. The guy has a handful of arrests and even a couple convictions for assault. From the length of time he spent in jail, it looks like he must have worked out deals with the prosecution."

"If he is connected with any element of organized crime, then he would have had access to some pretty good defense attorneys. Wheedling down the punishment is always easier than getting an acquittal, and it often suits both sides," I said.

"I always hated that," Rose said. "Did you have much of that in the military?"

"Fortunately, we didn't have a lot of crime in the air force, but I think plea bargaining is common no matter where you are."

"I can tell you that in El Paso, most of the cases that resulted in a conviction were plea bargains. It's like an automatic first step for the prosecution. Offer a deal and negotiate from there."

"I guess it makes sense for both sides."

"I know," Rose said, "but it gets frustrating when you work your butt off to give an open and shut case to the district attorney, just to have the guy walk off with a lesser sentence in a plea deal."

"So, we know Stinson is a violent man, but what is his motivation for these murders?" I asked.

"Who knows? I think we should pass the info on to Jerry and let his crew find out everything they can about Stinson's whereabouts when the murders occurred."

"Do it." She picked up the phone and called Jerry's office.

Chapter 20

"You aren't going to believe this," Rose said a few minutes later.

"Stinson confessed to the murders?"

"No, be serious. Stinson is the man who reported Sofi Puldark missing."

"The woman they're looking for?" I realized it was a dumb question as soon as I asked it. Her look at me confirmed it.

"Of course, they're going to call him back in for more questioning."

"That's too much of a coincidence," I said.

"We'll see."

"It seems to me that Jerry has a lot to look at right now, between interviewing the wedding party again because of Matt's lying to them and this guy Stinson, they're going to stay busy."

"Too busy if they're on the wrong trail," Rose said.

I nodded as the room phone rang.

Rose grabbed it and had a short conversation before hanging up. "We've been summoned again."

"Maybe they ought to move us to a cabin closer to their offices," I said when we were in the elevator. "So, no idea why they want us this time?"

"No, but at least they didn't sound angry."

"Why would they? Besides, my money is on your solving this for them."

"I hope you didn't put much money down on that bet," Rose

said. "My guess is that they want us to meet the new guys."

Her guess proved partially correct. We were ushered into an office and introduced to one of the three men who had arrived on the helicopter.

"Sinclair, this is Deputy Rose Luna from the El Paso County sheriff's office. She's the one I referred to in my briefs and whom we've identified to the Americans. She has been very helpful. Deputy Luna, this is Sinclair Mathison, our senior criminal investigator."

The two shook hands and said the obligatory nice to meet you. Mathison looked over at me and then back at Jerry.

"Oh yes, this is Mr. Jim West, her traveling companion," Jerry said.

"Her sidekick," I said.

"My friend," Rose said.

"Well, Mr. West it's nice to meet you, too" he said without much conviction. He was about five feet ten inches tall, a couple inches shorter than me, and had short cropped, gray hair. I took him for a few years older than me, maybe around fifty, but that would only be a guess. He wore a dark suit and tie with a white shirt rather than a ship's uniform.

"Please call me Jim."

"And I'm Sinclair."

Now that we were all good buddies, Jerry excused himself, and the three of us sat down at a small table. For the next twenty minutes, we discussed the investigation and our theories or lack thereof. Sinclair confirmed our belief that they were here to collect what they could from the crime scenes and to bring more manpower into the investigation. He didn't say more expertise, but his team's presence would do just that.

"We're looking at the missing woman as a separate incident from the two murders," Sinclair said towards the end of our meeting.

"Why is that?" I asked.

"We've got reason to believe that she met a man for drinks, no, I shouldn't put it like that. She picked up a man at one of our bars and left with him. From what our bartender has told us, she was drinking heavily and approached a man who was alone at the bar. According to our bartender, she was clearly the aggressive one."

"Do you know who this man is?" I asked.

"We're working it, but our theory is that when her boyfriend discovered she had been with another man, he killed her and threw her overboard. The background information you relayed to us just a little while ago added substance to our theory. He'll be interviewed again as soon as we can get him back in here."

"Makes sense," Rose said.

"He did seem to have a very short temper," I said.

"I assume you will be searching his cabin when you have him here," Rose said.

"Yes, would you like to take a look at it?"

"No, thank you, I'm sure you don't need my help."

"Maybe not," Sinclair said.

I couldn't tell, but I thought his voice carried a little bit of sarcasm.

"It will be great if you can find some connection between Lassiter and Stinson," Rose said.

"Yes, it would be, and we're working hard at doing that right now," Sinclair said. "We're also working hard trying to find out why the group of friends who came with the Lassiter couple, or what was a couple, have been misleading us."

"If I had a nickel for every time a person tried to cover for a friend, even when there was no need, I'd be rich," Rose said. "It's so stupid and messes up an investigation."

"They've told us a lot more this time. I don't know if they're frightened or simply fed up with each other. Lassiter's wife supposedly already had second thoughts about the marriage."

"They'd only been married one day," I said.

Sinclair shrugged, "And one of the men in the group was a lot more jealous than we knew before."

"Jealous of Lassiter marrying Sarah?" Rose asked.

"Yes."

"Crazy," she said.

"Unfortunately, all this simply leads us down a path to nowhere. They've all been cleared from doing the two murders. Their alibis are too good."

"Yes, but any of them could have hired someone else to do the killing," Rose said.

"We can see a financial motive for Mrs. Lassiter and perhaps for one of the men in the group, if he believed he could catch her on the rebound."

"Who is it?" I asked.

"I don't remember the name," he said.

"Well, I can't help but think we're wasting our time spending it on the wedding group," I said, not believing Sinclair couldn't remember the name.

"We don't have many other options besides this Stinson guy. We can make him for the woman's disappearance, but other than being from the New York area, we can't connect him to Lassiter," Sinclair said.

"Have you been able to do any more background searches on any of the people from New York?" Rose asked.

"I just got word that no one identified as being from the New York area works in the same company as the victim and none were immediate neighbors. Doesn't mean he didn't know one of them, but his friends couldn't identify any of them as someone they knew."

"If they're telling the truth," Rose said.

Sinclair nodded. "We know one of them has already lied to us about that. I don't think they'll lie to us anymore."

"What do you mean?"

"They may find this round of interviews a little more threatening. When a person realizes the absolute authority the captain of a ship has out at sea, it usually helps them to tell the truth."

"The sight of the gallows sharpens one's mind," I said, "or something like that."

"Correct," he said with a grin.

A knock at the door interrupted us. A man I didn't recognize looked in and held a piece of paper up for Sinclair to see. We were too far away to see what was printed on it, but Sinclair seemed to be waiting for it. He stood up saying he looked forward to talking to us later and walked out of the room.

"Think we can go?" I asked.

"I imagine so. It's not like we don't know our way out. He seemed like a nice enough guy. Hopefully, his team's presence will make the difference we need to catch the guy."

The door reopened before we reached it. The man who had held the paper up for Sinclair to see had returned to escort us out. When we got to the door that led out to the staff only area, we had to step aside to make room for two husky crewmen who were escorting Stinson into the area. Stinson saw me, and his face flushed with anger.

"You again," he said. "I imagine I have you to blame for this. We'll talk later." His voice was smooth and soft, but the air around me felt like I had suddenly stepped into a freezer.

Rose instinctively stepped in front of me.

Stinson smiled, "Later, when she isn't around to protect you."

One of the crewmen gave Stinson a shove, "Move on."

They went by us, and we walked out the door.

"Sorry about that," Rose said. "I don't know why I did that."

"You mean step in front of me to protect me?" I said, grinning.

"Yes, I didn't mean to embarrass you or imply you needed protection. That guy was threatening you, and I didn't like it. He reminded me of a rattlesnake. I guess you saw his eyes. Now I know where the term cold as ice comes from."

"Don't worry about it. I doubt if I see him again."

"Let's go back to our cabin." She wrapped my arm with hers and squeezed.

Chapter 21

"I can't believe I'm saying this, but I'm not that hungry," I said. About a third of the food I had piled on my plate sat untouched.

"Possibly because you took enough food to feed the entire Cowboys football team," Rose said.

We had spent an active forty-five minutes in our room before we decided on a late lunch, and I thought I was starving when we went through the buffet line.

"Maybe," I said. "I'm kind of at a loss to what more we can do to help catch this guy."

"After I finish this piece of pie, I want to go talk to Sarah again, by myself, if you don't mind."

"I don't mind at all. I need to go jog or walk a few laps, or perhaps, I should just take a nap."

"Go for the jog," Rose said and stuck a finger in my belly.

I compromised and decided I could walk one lap around the ship before I returned to the cabin for a nap. This was supposed to be a vacation after all. I took the stairs up to deck ten and gave serious consideration that the hike up the stairs could serve as sufficient workout. However, the warm sun and cool breeze invigorated me enough to stick with my plan.

I walked along the jogging path, being passed by the occasional jogger. About halfway around the track, two young women joggers ran by me. They wore matching, bright green and yellow, spandex body suits. I didn't get a good look at their faces, but after they passed by, they looked quite nice. I immediately thought a second lap couldn't hurt. Two crewmen ahead of me standing watch also seemed to focus their attention on the two women as they ran past them.

After four laps, the two women disappeared. I couldn't blame them since they had passed me at least eight times. I finished my fifth lap and stretched out on a recliner that someone had placed out of the wind in an alcove on the port side of the ship. Out of the breeze, the sun felt hot but good. I closed my eyes and thought about Rose. She had been a lot more passionate on the cruise than I had expected, not that I had any reason to expect any particular type of behavior. Our few days together before the cruise had forced a closeness that left me with the feeling that I knew her very well, yet I knew that feeling was only a feeling. No one could really know another person after only spending a handful of days together.

None of that mattered, I told myself. We were on this cruise, and I enjoyed being with her. I believed she felt the same way about me. My mind started to drift to what I should say or do at the end of the cruise. What did she expect? What did I want?

My eyes were shut, but I was awake while I thought. My focus on how to handle the end of the cruise stopped when I felt or sensed something blocking out the sun. The shadow lingered long enough that I opened my eyes in time to see Stinson jerk up the side of my recliner. I fell out but had enough warning to roll onto the deck and jump to my feet in one motion.

"Hey! Back off!"

He ignored me and stepped over the recliner. His right hand balled up into a fist, and I saw two large square-faced, metal rings on the fingers of that hand. He hadn't put them on for their looks.

Those rings could dice and slice a person's face if struck hard enough.

I moved to my right, out of the alcove, and away from his right fist. Hopefully, somewhere on this side of the ship, two crewmen would be standing watch with the primary goal of not letting someone else get murdered on this ship. I didn't have the luxury of looking around as Stinson closed in on me like a boxer cutting off the ring in pursuit of his opponent.

His first punch came straight at me. Not good, I thought, ducking down and away barely slipping the punch. A wild roundhouse would have given me some confidence that he didn't know what he was doing. True to his reputation, though, Stinson did know what he was doing. He feigned another punch with his right and drove his left into my gut. Fortunately, I was still backing away and avoided the full power of the punch, but the fist still hit me with a force that made me question the wisdom of the second piece of pie I had at lunch.

Stinson followed the left with another right, but this time I stepped inside of the blow. His fist grazed the side of my face, and I felt a scrape as the ring took some skin off my cheek when it went by. I tried to hit his nose with the flat palm of my right hand. I would have liked to have shoved it all the way back to his brain, but he was quick and deflected my hand at impact.

I wrapped my left arm around his right arm. "Calm down," I hissed.

He jerked his right arm away and stepped back a little off balance. I connected with a left jab that might have scored points in an amateur bout but did little to dissuade Stinson from continuing his assault. He had the gall to smile as he stepped closer and reached for me with his left hand.

I slipped to my right again, staying out of reach of his hand, and knowing that I had to do something quick to avoid my face being turned into sausage. I had boxed in college. Not by choice, but because as a freshman at the Academy you had little choice in what intramural sports you participated. The handful of upper classmen who loved the sport of boxing needed a fresh number of practice dummies each year to work their way through before the wing championships. Freshmen, like me, made perfect practice dummies. In the ring, I perfected one half of Ali's quote: I could dance like a butterfly. I could bob and weave with the best of them. One had to if not getting knocked unconscious was important.

The second half of Ali's quote: "sting like a bee" hadn't come as naturally and teaching it had not been a priority. I learned more about fighting later, but the most important thing I learned is that only a fool trades punches with an experienced fighter, especially if that person has two skin flaying, bone crunching rings on his fingers.

Outside the ring, fighting fair is a myth. Stinson didn't attack me with the mindset that he wanted to give me a fair chance. So, when he stepped forward, and I kicked his knee sideways, I didn't feel like I cheated.

He went down quickly but started to get up.

"Don't be a fool," I said and heard running behind me.

"Stop! Come here."

Turning, I saw two crewmen come to a running stop right behind me. I stepped away from Stinson who had settled back down in a sitting position on the deck. A ship's officer in uniform, a short woman with black hair and wearing glasses, ran up with another crewman. She looked at my face and gasped.

"Restrain them," she said.

"I was attacked," I said.

"We'll see," she said.

Stinson, an old hand at being detained, didn't say a thing. One of the men placed flex cuffs on me, while a second did the same thing to Stinson. The officer said something into her radio. After getting a response that I couldn't hear but she acknowledged, she took me by the arm and led me away. I didn't look back to see what was happening with Stinson. As long as they kept him away from me, I was fine.

We hadn't gone far before I saw a familiar face hurrying toward us.

"Mr. West, what happened to you?" Inga asked.

"I was attacked by that Stinson character."

"Your face," she reached up at my cheek with a handkerchief and blotted an area below my left eye. When she pulled it away, I saw a large smear of blood. "Remove the restraints," she said.

"But I was told --"

"Remove them. I will take responsibility." Inga blotted the blood on my face again while the plastic cuffs were being cut off. "What happened?"

"Stinson saw me in the security office when they brought him in. I imagine he guessed correctly that I was the one who turned him in. While I was napping in the sun, he attacked me." A white lie, I hadn't been napping, but my eyes had been shut, and it seemed like a good excuse to explain how he got the drop on me.

"Let's go see the doctor," she said.

"Is it that bad?" I asked.

"No, but it needs to be properly treated."

"Will it scar? I could use a manly dueling scar."

She looked into my eyes and smiled in a way that sent tingles up my spine, and I never considered myself the tingling type. "I like the occasional scar," she said.

As we went down the stairs, she told me she would leave me in the doctor's office, and that someone would meet me there to take my statement after the doctor finished with me.

The doctor's office was on deck three and seemed small for such a large ship. The doctor reminded me of the old doctor on the television show Gunsmoke. A friendly guy, he chatted all the way through the brief procedure, telling me that this cruise had been the busiest and strangest one he had ever been on in his twenty plus years of cruising. Not knowing I was in the loop, he never elaborated on why it was such a busy cruise. He thoroughly cleaned the wound on my face and finished up by placing three butterfly bandages along the wound to keep it closed.

"Might have a line there, but it shouldn't scar," he predicted. The phone rang when he was in the middle of patching me up. He didn't comment on the call until I was about to leave. "Can you believe I have to go to one of the confinement cells to tend to someone's knee? I tell you, it's time for me to retire." He turned to the nurse helping him. "Myrna, can you finish this?"

"Sure," Myrna said. She could have been the doctor's older sister and didn't say much. She inspected the bandages and cleaned what was left.

"On your way," she said when she was done.

I looked around for anyone interested in getting a statement from me but didn't see anyone. By the time I reached our cabin, I started to think I might not leave it again during the cruise. Staying in bed and ordering room service sounded like a perfect way to spend the next day and a half. I was not totally surprised Rose was not in the room. If she and Sarah were talking, it could be a while.

"What happened to your face?"

I woke with a start, and it took a second or two to get focused. Rose stood there looking concerned. "Sorry, I was out of it." I sat up and rubbed my face only to suddenly pull my left hand away. "Oh, yeah, Stinson attacked me when you left me all alone."

"What? Where?"

"I was up on the jogging deck doing some laps."

"Jogging?" she sounded skeptical.

"No, I would've but I had my walking shoes on, but I did several laps. I took a break and laid down on a recliner. I closed my eyes, and next thing I knew, Stinson flipped me out of the recliner and attacked me."

"Well, other than the cut and a little bruising you don't look any worse for wear."

"Hey, the guy had brass knuckles and one mean ass stare. You should have seen the look he gave me."

"Ok, quit with the joking. Are you alright?"

"Yes."

"Did he really assault you?"

"Yes."

"Did he really have brass knuckles?"

"Two big rings."

"That could still do damage," she said and studied my face again.

"So you were able to run away?" This time she was the one trying to keep the grin hidden.

"Actually, I wish I could've, but luckily he underestimated me, and I was able to kick his knee out of whack."

"Good for you," she leaned in and kissed me.

Chapter 22

"You're wasting your time," the voice in the Ed Anderson's head said.

"Go away," he said out loud and then looked around to make sure no one had taken the seat at the small table behind him.

"Where am I supposed to go?"

Ed didn't answer. Why should he? This other persona, The Wind, was no more than a creation of his mind. He would not acknowledge it. The screen filled with a new website discussing schizophrenia. Every website gave him hope. He would fight this illness. Yes, that's what it was, an illness. A few pills and zap, it would be gone.

The laughter erupted again in his head, and this time he had to fight to not laugh out loud. He had to stay in control.

"You can't get rid of me. I'm you. We both know you've been a coward too long. What would you have done just an hour ago when they were questioning you. You almost hyperventilated."

"No," he said out loud and again looked around. This time he noticed a woman across the room give him an inquisitive look.

The laughter again, and the voice in his head continued. "You know you panicked. You begged me to help. Over nothing, you fell apart over nothing. They knew Sofi left the bar with us."

Ed wanted to scream "there is no us," but he knew he did indeed panic. He hadn't known what to say when they knocked on his door and asked to come in. They had looked past him and into the room. He wanted to slam the door, to hide whatever they could see, but The Wind assumed control, and Ed had acquiesced.

"Please come in," The Wind had said, and the two ship's officers entered his cabin. "What can I do for you?"

The short officer, a red haired, stocky man looked around a second before looking at Ed. "Yesterday, we have reason to believe a Miss Sofi Poldark left the poolside bar and returned to this cabin with you."

"Yes, I'm afraid we had both been drinking, officer, but I assure you everything we did was consensual. If she or anyone is making an allegation that it wasn't, then it simply isn't true. She said she was traveling with a man who treated her badly. I cautioned her that maybe it wasn't a good idea, but she didn't want to hear it. If she's saying now that I took advantage of her, it simply isn't true."

"May we look around?" the officer had asked.

"Of course. Seriously, if Sofi is saying I took advantage of her, she's only doing so to protect herself against her boyfriend."

Their search had been cursory. "What time did she leave?"

"I'm not really sure. I fell asleep after it got dark, and when I woke she was gone. I glanced at the clock, and it was two something or other."

The two officers thanked him and left the cabin.

He knew now, as he had then, that The Wind had controlled his behavior and his answers. He had indeed acquiesced.

"You didn't acquiesce," The Wind roared in his mind. "You begged."

A tear came to his eye, and he pulled up a different website. Schizophrenia …….. How did it happen to him? His behavior had always been normal. People described him as a gentleman.

He had never been cruel to people or animals. How did this happen, he wondered. When did he first experience a feeling that someone else, no not someone, something else inside him was trying to control his behavior?

He clicked on a new website that discussed multiple personality disorder or dissociative identity disorder. What did it matter what they called it, Ed thought. He wanted to get rid of it. This couldn't be what he had; the article said it was normal for someone who suffered from this to have many different personalities, not just two.

"You think we have another one of us in here?" the voice in his head asked. "I don't like that either."

Ed shook his head, trying to clear it. The website claimed that the disorder was usually brought about by severe abuse as a child. He thought back to his younger life and even during his years of employment but couldn't think of a single incident of abuse or mistreatment. Not only that, he never wanted to hurt or kill anyone either.

But that wasn't true. After his former secretary told him that Lassiter had thrown away the coin, he had a strong desire to hurt Lassiter. In fact, he now recalled that he felt so mad upon hearing what Lassiter had done that he had a conversation with himself about what to do with Lassiter. It hadn't felt that strange at the time. He had voiced his thoughts out loud, that's all. Could that have been the first time?

From that point on, he researched and planned to kill Lassiter. He never questioned the need to kill Lassiter and never felt like someone or something forced him to do it. For the first time since that day, he questioned why he needed to do it. Why did he pick a plan to kill three people, and why did he kill poor Sofi?

It wasn't him, he told himself. For a moment he felt relieved.

"Oh sure, like anyone is going to believe that. The devil made me do it alibi has never worked to keep anyone from being convicted," the voice in his head said. "We did it together. You wanted to do it, but you needed me to be in charge. You even named me, remember, The Wind."

"No, that was only my imagination."

"Well, now I'm here, and I'm not going anywhere."

Ed closed his eyes and shook his head again. When he opened them, he clicked on another website. There had to be something here that could help. He looked around to make sure no one was watching him.

Had he become a Dr. Jekyll and Mr. Hyde? Did he have a multiple personality disorder? Could there be more personalities in him that he didn't even know about? Why hadn't he ever experienced similar things happening to him in the past?

Ed tried to think if he had bumped his head in the last year or two, but couldn't remember an incident that he could point to as an injury that might have resulted in his current condition. He hadn't experimented with any drugs and hadn't had a stroke or other serious health issue. Without knowing a cause, could he cure this ailment?

Maybe he had such a simple, structured life that this other persona in him had no reason to come out. That made sense to him, but didn't explain why being fired and the loss of the coin had such an impact on him.

No, Ed thought, that wasn't true. Being fired messed up his whole life, his plans for the future, and separated him from the only friends he had. When he learned Lassiter threw the coin in the trash, it felt like a hot poker pressing against an open wound.

Later, after discovering his firing had not been the result of management shuffling things around in an effort to make the company more efficient, but was done to bring a family member into the company, Ed's anger only grew.

The more he thought about it, Ed concluded that his firing must have been the catalyst for his dilemma. A short time after his firing, two final events occurred that started him on his path to wanting to kill Lassiter. First, the arrival of his letter of recommendation from Hudson Financial that he had hoped could help him gain future employment had referred to Ed only as an above average employee. Not good, not great, not valuable, not anything that might motivate a potential employer to hire him.

Finally, the tax grab that took over fifty percent of his separation package away left no doubt in Ed's that he had been screwed. By then, he had already taken the first few steps down the path to murder, but having this money virtually stolen from him ensured that there would be no exits from the path.

What good was knowing this? Ed thought. He had no regrets to killing Lassiter. He just wanted The Wind to go away.

Chapter 23

The cabin phone rang, and Rose answered it. She talked for a few minutes before hanging up. She had come from the shower and wore a sleek baby blue bathrobe. I would've told her she looked beautiful in it, except I'd already told her that three times on the cruise, and the last time she had reminded me that I had already complimented the robe twice.

I considered a different compliment like "hubba hubba," but decided against it, since I figured she already had enough evidence to question my sophistication.

"That was Jerry," she said and sat on the bed next to me. "He said not to worry, that they are going to keep Stinson locked up for the rest of the cruise. I think they've pretty well settled on him as the guilty party behind the woman's disappearance."

"He would get my vote, too. Did he say how bad his knee was?"

"No, he didn't comment on it. It could be because he doesn't care, or it could be that Stinson's knee is fine."

"I can't believe you didn't learn anything new from Sarah. Your interview techniques must be getting rusty," I said.

"I didn't say that I didn't get anything new, just nothing new that could help the investigation. She admitted that things weren't all perfect the first night on the cruise."

"Not that it matters anymore," I said. "I imagine a lot of newlyweds have adjustment issues."

"Did you?"

"Not that I can remember."

"Then why did you say that?"

I had a feeling that I had somehow walked myself into a corner and was about to give the wrong answer no matter what I said. "Oh, I don't know. I simply guessed it might be the case for some people."

She stared at me for a second. "Some men still consider a wife as property. They can be polite and compromising in a relationship, but change once they get married."

"I don't doubt it, but I imagine some women change, too."

Her stare got a little more intense.

"Okay, I sense I'm heading down the wrong path here. What am I saying wrong, Rose? I admit I'm no expert on relationships."

Her stare went away, replaced with a smile. "It's not your answers. I guess it's more on whose side you're on."

"Sides? I'm on your side." I couldn't imagine how that could be a wrong answer.

"Good, that's smart, but do you think a man owns his wife?"

"Of course not. They were only married for a little over twenty four hours. How could they have gotten to a point about who owns who?"

"It's an attitude," she said. "It doesn't take long to recognize it."

It finally dawned on me that Sarah must have said something about Lassiter's behavior that struck a sensitive nerve with Rose. I didn't know that much about Rose's past, at least where her prior relationships with men were concerned. I didn't want to know either.

"Does it give her a bigger motivation to kill hill him?" I asked.

"No, that's not my point. I'm just saying that she didn't realize how big of a jerk he was until that night."

I thought about different ways to respond, but I wasn't even sure what night she meant, so I decided to change the topic. "I wonder whatever came from the latest interviews of the wedding party."

"Nothing much, I guess. Jerry only said that they were no closer to solving the investigation than before."

"The trouble is that if we look who benefits from Lassiter's death and compare it with who is on this ship, the number comes down to only one or two. If we look at who may have a grudge against him, the number comes down to the same two. If we didn't know Sarah and her friends, we'd be trying harder to find out how they could've been behind the murder. Should we be doing that?"

"No," Rose said. "I guarantee that's exactly what Jerry's team has been doing since they found Lassiter, and that's what the reinforcements will be focusing on. "

"Did Jerry tell you that?"

"Not in so many words, but that's the feeling I've gotten from the start, and he did make the comment that they hadn't given up on them yet. I don't know, but I think we need to look elsewhere."

"Okay, I'm with you. I suggest we dig a little more into Lassiter's life. Has something happened in the last year or two that may have resulted in someone wanting him dead? Did he have an affair with someone's wife, gambling debts, ripped someone off, that kind of stuff," I said.

"Yes, did he drop a longtime lover for Sarah? Did he undermine someone's business or livelihood?"

"We're on a roll with ideas, but how do you suggest we get

any answers?"

Rose stood up and walked over to the window. She stared out at the water, "Let's get Sarah really involved in this, too. We've been treating her like a victim, which I think she is, but we need to push her past that and get her involved as an investigative reporter. She knows him better than us, obviously, and can help us fill in the blanks. Additionally, she may be able to get us access to all his social media stuff."

Part of me didn't want to go there. It seemed harsh with her husband barely dead for forty-eight hours, but I knew she was right. We'd never get to know Joe Lassiter in the short time we had left without her help. "Okay, sounds like a plan. Let's hope she'll go along with it."

"She has no choice if she wants Joe's murderer caught."

"It's late now, but Sarah has been alone in her cabin for most of the last two days. She may not want to sleep," I said. "Want to go over there now?"

"Yes, and I don't think we should call her first. She may be tired of seeing me."

"Rose, who could be tired of seeing you?"

She picked up her note pad from the dresser and we left our cabin. The same crewman whom we saw the first day guarding Sarah's cabin was there again. He recognized us and knocked on Sarah's door as we approached. She met us at the door.

"If you're here to try to talk me into leaving my cabin, forget it. I've already told my cousin that I'm not leaving," Sarah said.

She looked pretty ragged. I thought her hair needed to be brushed and a few hours sleep wouldn't hurt her either.

"Come on, Sarah, we need to get to work," Rose said and walked past her into the cabin.

Sarah looked at me, her eyes questioning what was up. I followed Rose into the cabin and took Sarah's hand as I walked by. "Come on, we need your help."

Rose sat down in one of the chairs and flipped open her note pad. "Sarah, we need to dig deeper. I need you to get us into anything and everything that might tell us more about Joe. Help us get into his social media, emails, texts, bank history, work history, anything and everything that might lead us to a motive and possibly a murderer."

"I don't how to do that?" she said.

"Then we'll help," I said.

"Let's start with the easy part," Rose said. "Do you know anything about his past girlfriends or relationships?"

"Some, but not much. He wasn't going with anyone when I met him. He's got money and always bragged that picking up women was easy for him. He claimed he could find a different one every night."

"Just boasting?" I asked.

"No, he was rich and handsome. In the city, there are lots of women looking for just that sort of man," Sarah said.

I almost asked her if she was one of those type women, but kept my mouth shut.

"Do you know if any of them were married?" Rose asked.

"If they were, I don't know."

"How about under age?" I asked.

"Who can tell these days," Sarah said, "but again, none that I know of. I always imagined he was quite the player, but I have no reason to believe he continued chasing other women after we got engaged. In fact, I'm pretty sure he hasn't. One of the guys would have told me."

"Any of these other women stalk him after he started seeing you?" Rose asked.

"No," she said. "At least not that I know of."

"Any issues with siblings that might be serious?" Rose asked.

"No, none at all. They're all alike."

"So no squabbling over inheritance or access to their parents' money," Rose asked.

"No. He was making good money at his new job."

"Any problems at his old job?" I asked.

"No, he didn't think it was very challenging, and when his uncle got him this one, he was happy about it. That was about the time we got engaged."

"No one in his old job hold a grudge against him for leaving? He didn't take a lot of clients or business with him when he left?" I asked.

"No. Like I said, he was bored there, and his uncle brought him into the new job and even restructured the position to make it a lot more than before. I guess he had to do that to justify the increase in salary," Sarah said.

"Did anyone lose their jobs when he came in?" Rose asked.

"I think one or two people were let go, but I'm not sure. Joe said that the section was not in good shape, that it was doing things the same way for fifty years and needed to be brought into the twenty first century."

"Did any of the people let go ever send any kind of threatening message to Joe?" Rose asked.

"Not that I know of. Joe said he needed to figure out a way to fire one of the old secretaries that was still there, but I don't think he had done so before we left."

"Did he have any issues with neighbors?" I asked.

"No," Sarah shook her head. "There's no one I know of who might have a motive to kill Joe. That's all I've been thinking about and I can't think of anyone."

"I know you're frustrated and angry and sad, but we need to do this. Do you have any suspicions either Joe or his family may have had anything to do with any criminal group or activity?" I had my friend Stinson in mind when I brought this topic up, but Sarah quashed right away.

"No," she said a little louder than necessary. "Do you think I would have married him if I knew of any?"

"Jim had a reason to ask that question. He had a little run in from a mob related character today," Rose pointed at my cheek.

"I meant to ask about that," Sarah said. "Sorry."

"No apologies needed," I said. "This guy Stinson is suspected of throwing his girlfriend into the ocean. He's from New York, has a history of violence, and is believed to be connected to the mob."

"They don't use that term anymore," Sarah said. "Do you think he killed Joe?"

"Unfortunately, no, but that's still being looked into," I said. "Can you get into his Facebook page?"

"Yes, but he never used it."

"Let's see it," Rose said.

"I've been through a lot of this already. One of the ship's people looked at it, too." She opened a drawer and brought out a Samsung phone. After a few seconds she handed Rose the phone. Joe's Facebook page was open.

"Give me a few minutes," Rose said.

Sarah looked at me for a few seconds. "The captain has comped the rest of the trip for me. Can I order you something from room service? If we're going to be doing this for a while, I need a drink."

I looked around the room but didn't see any evidence of alcohol in the room. "Sure, let's get something."

"I'm going to order a bottle of chardonnay. What do you want?" she asked.

"I'll have some of that, but we'll need to eat something with it," I said.

"Like what?"

"Oh, I don't know, how about pizza?"

"You'll have to eat it," Sarah said.

"Pepperoni," I said. I looked over at Rose, and she nodded. Sarah made the call.

"Do you know any of these Facebook friends?" Rose asked Sarah.

"A few, but I don't know of any of them who would want to harm Joe."

"I don't see anything here either. How about emails, personal and work."

"Click on the mail icon. His password for everything is IronMan23. Silly, I know, but I guess every boy has to have a superhero to idolize." Sarah looked at me.

"Not me, my Superman pajamas were a gift," I said and got a grin from both the women. "Did we ask if Joe had any gambling debts or did anyone owe him a lot of money?"

"I think you did, but no, I'm not aware of any debts or debtors. He even paid cash for his cars."

"Do you know if he changed his will to have you as his beneficiary?" I asked.

"I don't know if he even has a will," Sarah said. "Besides, a lot of what he has and the family has is tied up in a family trust."

Sarah and I talked a while about the trust and Joe's family. Rose continued through the emails and texts, every now and then looking up to ask a question.

"Sarah, do you know why he hasn't kept any of his older, personal emails? Most people never delete all the older emails," Rose said.

"I've always thought there might be things he didn't want me to see, but that was probably just my imagination. He said old emails only junk up the system and that there wasn't anything important in a personal email over a year old."

"He's probably right about that," I said. "Have you looked at his office emails?"

"Doing that now. I can't believe he used the same password for everything."

"Shouldn't be too much there either, since he's only been working there a little less than a year," Sarah said.

"I wonder if it's possible to get access to his email account from his former employer," I said.

"You need a warrant," Rose said.

"I know that, but can't you hack into it like they always do on television?"

Rose simply rolled her eyes at me.

"So, no hidden talents?" I teased.

"Sorry, Mac, you've seen everything I've got," Rose said.

I grinned and looked at Sarah for support.

"You don't want me to get involved in this discussion," Sarah said.

Room service knocked on the door and gave me a good opportunity to change the subject. I opened it and let the steward and his push cart in. We helped him transfer everything to the small table in the room, and I gave him a couple bucks when he left.

"I never know how much to tip on a cruise ship since everything you get at the bar or restaurants that cost extra gets a service surcharge put on it," I said.

"A couple extra dollars is always appreciated," Sarah said.

We drank wine and ate pizza. Sarah wanted to know what we thought of Cozumel, so I talked while Rose continued through the data in the phone. Maybe because of the stress or lack of food, but the wine seemed to affect Sarah more than Rose or me.

"The only thing the least bit contentious in any of the office emails is about Agnes, whom I'm guessing is the secretary Joe wanted to fire. I don't see a last name. Do you know it?"

"No," Sarah said. "I didn't even know her first name. Joe just complained about her that one time. Was she ever fired?"

"Good question," Rose said. "We need to follow up. If she was fired, and if that put her in a bad spot, some family member could be here seeking revenge."

"We need to compare a list of company employees with who is on the ship, and we need to find out if Agnes is still an employee. If she isn't, we need to identify members of her family," I said.

"I don't think Jerry has done that," Rose said. "Now that word is getting out, we need to get that list."

Sarah said, "Rose, go into his contacts on the phone. Give Sylvia a call, or better yet let me call her. She's Joe's assistant, or was." Her voice cracked when saying these last two words. "I've met her a few times."

Rose handed Sarah the phone and Sarah made the call. A

moment later she was crying while trying to talk to Sylvia. She apologized saying she thought she was over all the crying and after answering a few more questions got around to asking for a list of current employees.

"I realize it may be against company policy, but we need it to match with the cruise passenger list to eliminate anyone with the company being linked in any way to Joe's murder. We don't need anything but the names." She listened for a moment and looked at me and shrugged her shoulders. "They can, but if they do, it will become an official matter, and the police will get involved. I'm sure there's no match." This time when she looked up at me she crossed her fingers. "Oh, fantastic, no one else will know. Send it to me now, can you?"

She gave Sylvia her email address and thanked her two or three times more before saying she would call her once she got back onshore and had talked more with Joe's family.

"She'll download it and send it to me in a few minutes," Sarah said once she was off the phone.

"Thanks, Sarah," Rose said. "Sorry to put you through that."

"I thought I was done crying."

"It may take a long, long time," I said. "Even if we don't get a match with the passenger manifest, we'll be able to get an ID on Agnes."

"If she's still with the company," Rose said.

We finished the pizza and wine with Sarah getting the last glass of wine and I got the last piece of pizza. I offered to split the pizza with Rose, but luckily she said she didn't want any more.

"It's here," Sarah held up her phone. "Let me get my laptop." She stood up from the bed and staggered a little while walking the few feet to the dresser. "I think I drank that wine a little too fast." She opened the laptop and pulled up the email. Once she had the attachment open, she handed me her laptop. "Take a look, but I guess we ought to forward it to Jerry right away."

The list wasn't that long. Eighty four employees and fifth from the bottom I saw the name Agnes J. Wilson. "Here she is," I said and pointed at the name. Rose had come over and was looking over my shoulder.

"I got it," Rose said, and I saw that she had written the name down. "Let's do send it off to Jerry."

"You should probably call him and tell him it's coming," I said and handed the laptop back to Sarah.

Someone knocked on the door. Sarah said, "I wonder who that could be," and went to the door.

Her cousin, Jill, stood there with a bottle of wine in her hand. "I'm coming in," she said emphatically and walked into the cabin. "Oh, I didn't know you had company."

Chapter 24

"What ya all doing?" Jill said, sounding a little like the wine bottle in her hand wasn't the first she had handled that night. "If I knew you had company, I would've gotten dressed."

Jill wore a white bathrobe that had the cruise line logo on it. I figured she had something else on under it but not much. She smiled at me.

"Hi, Jill, we're just here brainstorming what else we can do to help ship's security catch whoever killed Joe." It sounded too blunt after I said it, but when I looked at Sarah she didn't seem to be fazed by my remark.

"I want to help," Jill said. She sat down on the bed, crossed her legs, and held the bottle out in my direction. "Jim, will you pour us all some wine."

I took the bottle and went in search of another glass. Rose was on the phone talking to Jerry but managed to nod her head, which I took for agreeing to have another glass of wine. I poured everyone some wine and set the bottle down next to the empty one on the dresser.

"Jerry said he will have someone compare the two lists tonight, so before we drink too much more wine, we'll need to send this list to him," Rose said.

"Just forward it from my email," Sarah said. "It's open."

I gave the laptop to Rose, and she forwarded the list before setting the laptop down on the small table.

"How can I help?" Jill said, looking at me.

"I'm not sure," I said. "How much trouble are the boys in for not coming clean with the ship's security?"

"You mean Matt? He's the only one who didn't tell them everything," Jill said.

"Yes," I said.

"I don't know, but he and his two buddies have been assigned another cabin down below somewhere and can't leave it tonight," Jill giggled. "He's so stupid."

"That he was for not mentioning his two friends, when he first reviewed the list. He knew they were on the cruise all along. There's no reason to think they were involved with anything, is there?" Rose asked.

"No, no way. They may have known Joe, but Matt is one hundred percent sure they weren't involved," Jill said.

Rose rubbed the scar that her hair covered, exposing it for a second.

"What happened?" Jill asked as she stared at Rose' forehead.

"Oh," Rose said, covering her scar with her hair. "I guess you can call it a job related injury."

"Looks like it happened recently," Jill said.

"It's her newest beauty mark," I said, trying to lead the discussion away from a topic I believed Rose still didn't want to talk about. "Did either of these two guys work with Joe?"

"No, I don't think so," Jill said. "Matt knew them during his college days. They were all going to go scuba diving together, something I didn't know." She scooted back on the bed against the head board and stretched her legs out, raised both arms stretching them over her head, and yawned. In doing so, she exposed a little more of herself than my mother would have thought appropriate. She noticed me staring and smiled at me.

I thought I heard my name being called the first time, but I was seriously being distracted. When Rose said my name for the second time, I looked at her.

"Are you going to be okay?" she asked, and the other two women giggled.

I nodded and thought I saw the hint of a grin on her face and figured she was also enjoying my discomfort.

"How about if I sit there," she said.

I stood and let her take the chair, while I leaned against the dresser.

Jill started pressing Sarah to leave the cabin tomorrow as it would be our last day at sea. Rose had her phone out and texted some one. A few seconds later my phone buzzed in my pocket. I took it out and saw that Rose had sent the text to me. "Why don't you head back to the cabin. You've got Jill all wound up, and I'd like the chance to talk to them alone. They may be more chatty now."

I felt a little like I was being dismissed, which I didn't like. I looked at Rose, but she was already laughing with the other two women about something. Sarah had scooted over on the bed and now lay there with her head propped up on one arm. She looked more at ease now than she had at any earlier point on the cruise. Even now, with her hair a mess and no makeup, she was a pretty woman. Side by side, Jill and Sarah's family relationship stood out. Jill could easily be taken for her sister.

"No! I'm not going for spa day, I couldn't," Sarah said.

"Come on," Jill said.

"Maybe it's too soon," Rose said in support of Sarah.

I realized I didn't need to be there any longer. "I've got to run, but before I do, can I top off anyone's wine?"

Jill raised her glass right away.

"Might as well," Rose said and held her glass up.

Sarah looked hesitant, but the peer pressure got to her. I emptied the bottle into their three glasses.

"Can't you stay?" Jill said. "We can all play games."

I was a little disappointed neither Sarah or Rose supported Jill's request, but I knew it was time to escape. Rather than head back to the cabin, I went in search of coffee and, if I was lucky, a piece of toast. I passed two crowded and loud bars before I found a small stand out on the deck that displayed coffee and small pieces of cake, brownies, and pie. Four outdoor tables provided a place to sit, and what I thought was Plexiglas shielded the space from the wind.

A lone man sat at one of the tables, and a very tall crewman swept the deck floor around the coffee stand.

"Good evening," I said.

The crewman smiled back at me. He placed the broom against a wall, "Coffee?"

"Yes, but I can…"

Despite it being a self serve station, the crewman grabbed a cup, filled it for me, and put the coffee on a tray. "Cake?"

"The white cake," I said.

He placed a plate with an already square cut piece of white cake with white frosting on the tray next to the coffee.

I thanked him and sat down at the nearest table. He went back to sweeping.

Coffee made by the gallons and served in large metal pots has never really impressed me, and this coffee had cooled. The cake, on the other hand, had somehow stayed moist and tasted good.

One had to give the cooks on these big ships credit.

A nearby conversation broke the relative silence around me. I looked around and other than the man sitting about ten feet away from me and the lone crewman, I saw no one. I dismissed the conversation thinking some people must have walked by in the shadows. A few seconds later, I distinctly heard the man at the table say no and then something else I couldn't make out.

I've been known to talk to myself, especially on the golf course, but this guy wasn't playing golf. I knew there could be more than a few reasons why a guy might carry on a conversation with himself, but I still found it kind of spooky. He slammed his fist down on the table, stood up, looked around like he hoped no one had noticed, and hurried away. For the most part, I tried not to look at him, as I felt he was embarrassed.

After he left, the crewman came up to me. "More coffee or cake?"

"No thanks. Had that guy been there long talking to himself?"

"Yes, he strange," the crewman said.

I nodded and the crewman walked away. My mind went back to Rose, Sarah, and Jill. I didn't necessarily want it to, but I seemed to have little control over all the silly things that were flying through my mind. Finally, I focused on the next step I wanted to pursue in Joe's murder. I wanted to talk to Agnes. She had to know that Joe was out to fire her, and even if she was still employed, there might be enough bad blood between them for her to tell me all the gossip or derogatory stuff she had on him.

The call couldn't be made until morning, so I walked a lap around the ship to let the fresh air work with the coffee to help the day's take of alcohol work through my system. Most of the crowds had already dissipated, but small clumps of rowdy people refused to let the late hour or the news of murder keep them from having their fun. I passed a half dozen pairs of crew personnel keeping vigil in the night.

Back in the cabin, I took a shower and sent a text to Rose that I was going to bed. She replied that she might be a while. Before falling to sleep, I found myself hoping Rose wouldn't be too late. My mind, however, couldn't focus on Rose and kept sending me the vision of Jill stretching out on that bed. She was still smiling at me and seemed to be purring like a cat. I hoped my thoughts didn't reflect some serious character flaw but rather some typical male reaction to stimuli.

Chapter 25

I fell asleep trying to organize my thoughts, but what woke me at two in the morning had nothing to do with the three women or the call to Agnes. A thought developed somewhere in my subconscious and had broken through to me that the man I observed talking to himself looked and moved like our suspect in the video.

The light I left on in the bathroom for Rose provided enough light to look around. Rose hadn't returned. I got out of bed and checked my phone, but it displayed nothing but the time: two o'clock. I considered calling Sarah's room but decided to let them be. Instead, I went out on the balcony where a cool soft breeze greeted me. We must have a trailing wind, I thought, and sat down.

I tried to remember the man's face, but I hadn't really seen much of it. I had looked down at my coffee when he got up and walked away, because I thought he was embarrassed. Besides, I had no need to stare at him. I caught a glimpse of his profile and watched him walk away. That was it. I wondered if in my sleep, I simply created a false connection.

On the dark horizon, I saw another ship passing by to the south and felt a little cheated out of a normal cruise with Rose. I started to imagine what it could have been like when my mind, like it was on autopilot, went back to the man at the table talking to himself. He wasn't simply talking, he was arguing with himself. So what? What's the difference, I thought but couldn't come up with a quick answer.

The fresh air kept me wide awake for a while, but finally I decided to head back to bed a little aggravated that Rose had not returned.

A minute or two later, the door to the cabin opened. "Rose?" I asked.

"Yes, were you hoping for someone else?"

"How did everything go?" I asked, ignoring her question.

"Okay, we can talk in the morning."

A few minutes later, I felt Rose crawl into bed.

"Why are you so cold?" she asked.

"I've been out on the balcony. I have something I want to talk about, too. I stopped out on the deck, up by the front of the ship, for some coffee and saw this guy talking to himself."

"Hmmm," Rose murmured.

"It was strange." I stopped talking. She had fallen asleep.

My mind remained active for some time despite my efforts to fall asleep. I tried to stop thinking about the man, but he kept popping back up, and at one point, I wondered if he was talking to me. Sleep finally snuck up on me.

Sunshine invaded the room much earlier than it should have. In the darkness of the night before, I forgot to close the blackout curtains. I got up and closed them.

"Thanks, but I'm awake," Rose said.

"How do you feel?"

"Okay, except my head hurts a little. Drank more wine than I'm use to. Sorry I was out so late, but Jill is quite the talker, and she eventually got Sarah to open up and talk."

"Anything new that can help us?"

"No," Rose said. "I snuck in a few questions when I could, but I'm pretty convinced they know nothing that can help us and had nothing to do with Joe's death."

"Let's not waste any more time with them."

"At all?" Rose asked.

"No, no, I only mean as far as the investigation goes."

"This is the last day of the cruise. I almost think we should forget the investigation. I'm sorry I got us involved," Rose said.

"Nothing is your fault," I said. "We'll get a response from Jerry this morning, I assume, and we'll call Agnes. Beyond that, I think we're stuck. Oh, I did have an interesting thing happen to me last night."

"What?"

"I stopped at a coffee stand last night out on the deck, and there was a man sitting not far from me who was arguing with himself. I didn't think too much of it at the time, but later I started thinking he looked and walked like our suspect."

"I didn't think there was a good shot of his face in any of the videos I saw," Rose said.

"There wasn't, but the profile seemed similar. The trouble is I didn't see this guy's face either."

"Any way you think Jerry's people can identify who he was?"

"I doubt it. You don't have to buy the coffee or cake, so there would be no record of him being there. It's probably a waste of time to bring it to Jerry's attention."

Rose climbed out of bed and went to look at her phone. "Damn. No matches between the list of employees and the passenger list."

"Maybe it was just some crazy guy after all," I said, and my mind went back to the man I saw the night before.

"Let's go get some breakfast," Rose said.

"Come here first," I said and held out my hand. She joined me back in bed.

Chapter 26

Ed woke with a start. He looked around the room and didn't see anything out of place. He felt damp and realized he had sweated throughout the night. Nervously, he stood up and looked around the room again. His mind struggled to remember the night before. What he could remember terrified him.

He spent most of the prior afternoon trying to learn more about schizophrenia or multiple personality disorder. More importantly, he spent most his time trying to find a way to cure it. By early evening his frustration peaked, and he began talking to himself again. He tried to be discreet, but he noticed people glancing his way at dinner and at the bar. At least the man at the coffee station last night had the courtesy not to stare at him.

"I'm going to see a doctor as soon as I get back home," Ed had told his other persona when he left the coffee station.

"You can't get rid of me," the Wind whispered. "I am you."

"No you aren't," Ed had said and noticed a couple cuddled under a blanket on deck chairs look up at him.

"I think I have more control than you now. Watch this."

But he couldn't, and that was the whole point wasn't it? After the Wind spoke the words "watch this," he couldn't remember a thing that he might have done the night before until he woke up a few minutes ago. He didn't even remember returning to his cabin.

Ed turned on the water to his shower and studied his hands and arms. At least he didn't see any blood.

"Ha! You think I'm stupid enough to leave blood on my hands," the voice in his head spoke to him again.

"Get out!" he screamed. "They're not your hands!"

"Maybe you should leave," the Wind whispered. "I'm enjoying myself. You should have seen the young lady last night. Maybe I'll share some of it with you, but no, maybe not. You seem to have such an aversion to blood this morning."

"What? What did you do? My God, what did you do?" Ed said and stepped into the shower hoping to clear his mind.

"You mean what did we do?" the Wind asked.

"There is no we!" Get out of my head!" Ed shouted.

"What do you want to see? How about this?"

A vision suddenly appeared in his mind of his hands dripping with blood.

"No!" Ed howled.

"Or how about this?"

A different image popped into his mind. In this one he was making love to a young woman he thought he recognized from somewhere on the cruise.

"So this one's okay. Keep watching," the Wind said.

Without warning, Ed saw his hands reach for the woman's throat and start choking her.

"No," Ed said, his voice straining.

"Oh, but you liked that one, didn't you?" The vision faded away.

"No, you must go away. Find someone else to torment," Ed pleaded.

"Didn't you enjoy watching what we did last night? Should I show you more?"

"Go away!"

"What do you think I am? Some alien from outer space? You fool, I am you. No, I am the real you. You have always been a coward. You don't deserve to exist. Maybe you're right, there is no we. It's just me, and the coward named Ed needs to go away."

"No, you are a disease, a malfunction, a psychological impairment. You don't exist, and I will find a way to get rid of you," Ed said.

Without a thought, Ed stepped out of the shower and walked toward the balcony. He felt strange, like he didn't have control of his movements. Confused, he opened the heavy, sliding glass door and put his left hand on the side of the stationary window, gripping it. He slammed the sliding door shut, or what would have been shut if his hand wasn't there.

Screaming, Ed collapsed to the floor, holding his injured hand.

"Don't ever think you're in charge again," the Wind whispered.

"No, no," Ed moaned and rocked on the floor in pain. Over his moans, Ed thought he could hear laughter.

Chapter 27

"Hello, Agnes?" I asked over the phone.

"Yes, this is she."

"Agnes, I'm Jim West. I'm calling on behalf of Sarah Lassiter and in cooperation with cruise line security. I believe you are aware of what happened to her husband Joe Lassiter."

"I only heard yesterday late afternoon. It's terrible."

"Yes, it is. We've already called and talked to a few other people whom he worked with there in New York. We're trying to find out any information that might lead us to a motive for anyone wanting to harm Joe."

"I'm not sure how I could help you," Agnes said.

"What can you tell us about Mr. Lassiter?"

"I didn't know him that well."

"What type of person was he? Like was he the type that offended people easily?"

"Well, now that you mention it," Agnes said, "he was a little abrasive. If you didn't agree with him, he thought you were stupid, and he didn't have any empathy for other people's problems."

"Can you be more specific?" I asked.

"I hate to speak poorly about him, now that he, well, you know."

"I do, and I understand, but it's important we get a complete picture of Joe."

"Yes, I guess you do. Well, for example, just a week ago, Sandra, that's Mrs. May, had to leave early to pick up her son at school, and Mr. Lassiter yelled at her in front of everyone that she had better get her priorities straight if she wanted to keep her job."

"You're kidding."

"No, he has very bad people skills. I mean had," she said and paused for a second. "He infuriated poor Ed."

"How so?"

"Ed was let go as part of the reorganization when Mr. Lassiter came in."

"And that made him mad at Joe?"

"No, not at first, of course he was devastated at being forced out. He had been with the company a very long time, even before me. A quiet man but very diligent and polite."

"So how did Joe aggravate Ed?"

"When Ed left, he forgot to take a commemorative coin that he had received from the Navy Seals or Army Rangers. I'm not really sure what military unit. I've seen it, and it was impressive. Ed was very proud of it. He called me a couple days after he left and asked me to get it, saying he would come by and pick it up."

"And what happened?"

"I guess Mr. Lassiter saw it in a box of stuff that was removed from Ed's desk and took it. He must have known it was Ed's, but he gave it to a client, and told me to lie to Ed by saying it was thrown out with the trash. Mr. Lassiter said I was specifically not to tell Ed that he had given it to a client, because he didn't want Ed trying to get it back from the client."

"And that's what made Ed mad?"

"Yes. I think he had also talked to someone else with the company by then, because he had found out Mr. Lassiter was related to one of the partners. That bothered him, too. Poor Ed.

Everyone liked him and being dismissed like that really got to him over that first month or so. I hope he's over it now and has found something else to keep him busy."

"Do you have Ed's phone number?" I asked.

"I'm sure I do somewhere, but I'll have to look for it. His last name is Anderson, Edward Anderson. I can call you back with his number."

"I'd appreciate that, Agnes. How about you? Did you have reason to dislike Mr. Lassiter?"

"Well, he's not a very pleasant… Oh my, I keep thinking he's still alive." The phone remained silent for a moment. "He was hard to work for, but I've had to work with worse in the past." Silence again for a good five seconds. "Are you still there Mr. West?"

"Yes, I'm here. I was just trying to get a good picture of Joe in my mind. Do you know if he had any financial problems?"

"I wouldn't know, but I wouldn't think so. His family is fairly wealthy, and he always wore expensive suits. I'm sorry I haven't been much help. I do hope you catch whoever did it."

"One more question, Agnes, was he trying to have you fired?"

"He was recommending a further reorganization that would have resulted in my position going away, but I have an old friend who said she could use me downstairs. So if my position was cut, it would be more like a transfer for me."

"Too bad Ed didn't have a fallback like that," I said.

"Yes, poor Ed, such a nice man. I think it has really devastated him."

"I really would like to talk to him. Please do call me or text me with his number."

She said she would, and I ended the call and looked over at

Rose. She had been in the bathroom getting ready for breakfast and had come out for the last part of the call.

"Is there an Edward Anderson among the passengers? He was fired when Lassiter was hired. He also stole a souvenir coin that belonged to Ed."

"Joe stole it?" Rose asked.

"Yes. It was among some stuff left behind in Ed's desk. Ed called Agnes for her to save it for him, but when Lassiter saw it, he took it and told her to tell Ed it was thrown out in the trash."

"And since Anderson is no longer with the company, his name wouldn't have been on the list of employees we have," Rose said.

"Right."

"Let me check," Rose said, and I finished getting dressed. Neither act took too long. "There are three Andersons on the list, but no Edward or Edwin Anderson. Two of the Andersons are from the New York area. Of these two, one of those is from New Jersey and other is from Pennsylvania."

"Pennsylvania? He'd have to live on the state line to be considered in the New York City metro area."

"I don't recognize the name of the Pennsylvania town," Rose said, "but it could be."

"But no Edward?"

"No, nada, but maybe it's a middle name."

"Possible, we'll have to run these two down. Where is the third one from?"

"Texas, but you know, if Anderson was fired a few months ago, he may have moved. Without a job, why stay in New York where it's so expensive?"

"Okay, we'll check all three of these," I said.

"There's also a Henderson. Did she spell out Anderson for you?"

"We only have one day."

Rose laughed at me. "Okay, we'll stick with the Andersons."

"No, you're right. We should take a look at Henderson, too. It wasn't the best connection, and I should have clarified the spelling and whether Ed might have been his middle name. Want me to call her back?"

"Unless you want me to," she said.

I redialed Agnes' number, but this time it went into voice mail. I didn't leave a message, since she was going to call me back with Ed's phone number, and I could always call again.

"Let's go eat before they run out of food," I said.

"Want to see if Jerry wants to join us?"

"I guess we should."

Rose called his office and left a message with one of the staff.

"He's already working, but the man who answered said he would relay our message to him," Rose said.

"Want to go to the dining room and get waited on or back to the buffet?" I asked.

"Let's go to the dining room. Maybe we'll eat less for once."

Rose and I left our cabin and took the stairs down to the dining room. My mind had gone back to the man I had seen the previous evening talking to himself.

"Everything okay?" Rose asked.

"Yes, I was just thinking about that man I saw. I keep thinking I made a critical error by not getting a good look at his face."

"You know that's silly. A few thousand passengers on the ship and you're thinking that the one person you encounter is the one we're looking for. What would be the odds?" she said.

"I know, but look at this another way. We've run across a thousand people already by walking around the ship or staying at one spot and watching people go by. At some point, we should bump into the killer."

"Well, it's too late now, and what would you have done anyway?"

"I could've tried to talk to him, get to know who he was," I said.

"If he was the killer, he would've given you a false name, an incorrect cabin number, anything but his real name," Rose said.

"Maybe."

The breakfast crowd in the dining room occupied less than a third of the tables, and the hostess sat us at a table next to a window. We sat next to each other to take advantage of the view of the water.

"So nothing at all came out of your visit with the ladies last night?" I asked.

"Not really. I'm more convinced than ever that Sarah and Jill have no clue at all as to what or who could've been behind Joe's murder. And, I'm pretty sure none of the other wedding party members had anything to do with it."

"Then we're no better off than before, and tonight, let's spend it together and away from that crowd. Deal?"

"Yes. Jill had way too much wine, by the way. Twice she asked me how serious our relationship was and suggested I stay the night in her bed, so she could surprise you in our cabin. I was tempted to say yes to see how you would handle it."

"No you wouldn't," I said.

She laughed. "No, I wouldn't, but what would you have done?"

"I would've kicked her out of the room, but in the dark, it might've taken me thirty or so minutes before I was sure it wasn't you."

"Men," she said. She started to say something else but saw Jerry approaching us.

We stood and asked him to join us.

"For coffee only," he said.

"I hope last night was a quiet night," I said, thinking that he didn't look like he had gotten any sleep.

"Yes, thankfully, no incidents of note. No more reports of missing people or even any loud noise complaints."

"People are scared," Rose said.

"I think so, too. Rumors have spread like wildfire. Oh, one thing of note, over a hundred steak knives disappeared from last night's dinner alone," Jerry said.

"For protection," Rose said, and Jerry nodded. "What do you bet most of the knives will be left behind in their rooms when they depart the ship?"

"I imagine you're right. I just hope they don't have a need for them while they are on the ship or stab some innocent person in a panic. Rather than produce anything new for us, the team of visiting experts has been going over everything we've done in this investigation. Trying to help, they say. I have a feeling they are trying to fix blame."

"Did they look at the crime scenes?" Rose asked.

"Yes, but they didn't do much but look. As expected, they said with the wind out on the deck, the scenes had been too contaminated to collect fibers, hairs, you know."

We did. "What's the feedback so far?" I asked.

"What they say to us doesn't really matter. What they report up the chain does, and we aren't privy to that," Jerry said.

I shook my head. "I can't see how they can hold anyone on this ship accountable for the actions of some crazy passenger."

"Right or wrong, it's all about our public image. We already have been notified that the captain will not be with us when we leave Galveston. We'll get a temporary skipper. I'm surprised they haven't recalled me, too."

"At least we have something different we can look into today. Another long shot but Lassiter's hiring a few months ago at Hudson Financial caused a long term employee to get fired. Lassiter further irritated this guy by stealing a commemorative coin of some sort. The guy's name is Ed Anderson, and since he's no longer employed by the company, he wasn't on the list we received from them. However, there are three Andersons on the ship," I said.

Jerry perked up a little. "Any of them an Ed, Edward, or Edwin?"

"No," Rose said, "but Ed could be a middle name or a nick name."

"I'll get them all in this morning. Rose, Jim, either of you want to watch?"

"Sure," Rose said. "There's also one Henderson. Could you include him?"

"My fault," I said. "I got the names over the phone and didn't verify the spelling. I've got a call back, but in the meanwhile." I shrugged my shoulders and showed the palms of my hands.

"Not a problem. What's one more when we are sitting around waiting for a break? Our own efforts have narrowed our search down to six hundred and thirty two."

"What do you mean?" Rose asked.

"One of the first steps we should've done, according to the team of experts. It's the number of white male passengers between the ages of thirty five to fifty five we have on the ship," Jerry grinned.

"A statistic for the statisticians," I said. "Brings you no closer to solving the case."

"Exactly," Jerry said. "If we had a lot more resources and a lot more time, we could whittle through that number, but with our constraints, knowing it doesn't help. By the way, the guy who assaulted you still claims he had nothing to do with his girlfriend's disappearance. My people are thinking that maybe he didn't do it."

"Could be," Rose said, "but I would expect him to deny it. He knows you don't have any evidence or a body."

"I know, but he's made a fairly good case that this trip with her was a last minute lark. He has no intentions of making any commitment to her and believed she felt the same way," Jerry said. "In fact, he has very little remorse that she is gone."

"Makes sense to me," I said and stifled a grin.

Under the table, I felt Rose give my ankle a soft kick. "If you hadn't already had the ship searched for her, I could see her finding a different guy to end the cruise with. Makes sense to me, too. We girls do make mistakes."

This time I had to smile.

"Am I missing something?" Jerry asked.

"No, she just has a bad sense of humor," I said and immediately felt another kick to my ankle.

"Well, I'll let you two sort things out," Jerry said and stood up. "I'll arrange to have the Andersons available at my office at ten this morning. It's a long shot, killing someone over a coin, but stranger things have happened. Will you two still be together by then?"

"I hope so," I said, and Rose looped her arm around mine.

Jerry walked off, and our server brought us more coffee.

Chapter 28

Ed's heart jumped when his cabin phone rang. He didn't answer it. He felt sick. Over the past hour he had slowly gotten his memory back from the night before. It hadn't returned in the normal sense of someone remembering something. Ed had fought hard to get to the truth and was still a little uncertain if what he recalled was accurate. He worried that this other persona in his mind, The Wind, had fed it back to him in stages and had given him visions mixed with both fact and fiction.

Ironically, the pain from his smashed hand brought back the first flashes of what had happened the night before. From there it was a test of wills between the two personalities fighting for control of Ed's mind. Visions of macabre brutality kept flying in and out of his mind. The sheer number of these terrible visions of his stabbing and slicing different victims, mostly young women, caused his usually rationale mind to realize he could never have done all these things. That kernel of logic helped him slowly unravel what was otherwise an uneventful night.

True, he had stolen a knife from a restaurant, and he had followed a teenager around for a while before she joined her parents and went somewhere with them, but nothing bad had happened. Still, the thought that something had driven him to follow a teenager around the ship both angered and scared him.

He came on the cruise to kill Lassiter. Killing the other two came with the plan. He regretted killing Sofi; however, he could see how it fit into his plan. A plan he knowingly set in motion. But now, stalking a teenager, visions of violence, seriously hurting his hand, these actions were not part of his plan. Worse yet, he had no control over these actions.

Ed left his cabin and went out on the deck searching for a place where the morning sun and the sea breeze might help him stay focused and in control. He found a semi private area on the tenth deck in the front of the ship. The cool breeze competed with the warm sun. Without meaning to, Ed began to identify with the sun's rays as they struggled to warm him against the chill of the wind. He felt some satisfaction a few minutes later, when his body warmed with the sun.

If he could only find a way to lock himself in his room or even out here on the deck, he thought. He didn't want to hurt anyone else. The voice in his head had remained quiet since he had left his cabin. Maybe it didn't like the sun. No, that made no sense; he had lured Sofi back to his cabin before the sun had set. But had that been The Wind? Couldn't he have done that without the involvement of this demon inside him?

Ed didn't give this theory much credence but decided to stay where he was for as long as he could. Safer here in the sun and away from other people, safer for him and for them, he thought. He entertained the idea of moving to a small island in the Caribbean or South Pacific. He had seen those television shows of people buying their own island, but those required money he didn't have. Maybe one of those atolls in the Pacific where they tested the atom bomb could be bought on the cheap. The thought made him smile.

"Twenty four hours," Ed said out loud. If he could only remain in control for twenty four hours, he could get off the ship and go to the nearest hospital.

Straight to a hospital, yes, that was what he would do. He

needed to be sedated until they could find a cure. After another fifteen minutes of sunshine and solitude, Ed began to wonder about that word "cure" and reconsidered his circumstances. He had killed Lassiter and the other two, so he had completed his original plan. Perhaps, in a way, he was now cured. He had lost control last night, but nothing had happened. He began to wonder if the visions of brutality could have been this other persona tormenting him. The Wind did not have a reason to kill or hurt anyone else, but did it need one?

Ed had not wanted to hurt Sofi, but he had to admit, his original plan included killing three people. Maybe this other persona, The Wind, only did what Ed wanted him to do. Was it possible that he actually did want to kill Sofi to fulfill his plan? Had he subconsciously allowed or encouraged this other piece of him to carry out the murder?

In an unexpected way, this theory had a calming effect on him. Perhaps The Wind wasn't something that he couldn't control, but rather a weapon that he could wield when needed. The loss of memory, however, concerned him. How could he be in control, if he couldn't know what he was doing as he was doing it? Maybe that was where a doctor or drugs could help him.

His mind kept running in circles until the need to use a restroom eventually forced him out of his sanctuary and back to his cabin. Coming out of his bathroom, Ed noticed the message light blinking on his cabin phone. He listened to the message which was a request by a ship's officer for him to come to the reception desk on the fourth deck.

Panic grabbed him, and he fought to control it. There was no way they could link him to any of the murders. He had spent hours going over everything he had done and couldn't think of any loose ends he may have left out there to be discovered. Besides, he thought, they had already searched his room and had talked to him about Sofi. If they thought he was the killer, would they call him and invite him down for a chat? More likely, they would come in force and get him. So, what could they want now?

He decided to ignore the request for now and wondered where he could go on the ship to stay out of sight for as long as possible. No matter what they wanted to talk to him about, Ed believed he needed to delay any further interviews. The less time left on the cruise would mean the less time they would have to follow up on any lies he might have to tell.

Chapter 29

Shortly before noon, the first of the Andersons showed up, and Rose and I had the opportunity to observe him while they brought him to the interview room. He looked in his mid to late twenties, younger than my impression of the killer. He also appeared more curious than concerned.

"Not him," Rose said.

"I agree."

They didn't keep him long, and he left still looking more curious than concerned.

Jerry approached us after the first Anderson left. "Don't think it's him," he said. "The guy was all smiles and ignorance. I've been played before, but he doesn't fit."

"He looked younger than the guy you caught on camera." I said.

"That, too. We haven't made contact with the others, but we now have eyes on each of their cabins."

One of the new arrivals who came in by helicopter to help with the investigation entered the room. I didn't think we had been introduced.

"Jerry, an American law enforcement team will be meeting with us tomorrow when we approach Galveston harbor. They'll come out with the harbor master. Will you have a briefing arranged for them?" the new guy said.

"Certainly, does the skipper know?"

"Yes, and he suggested they be present for the briefing," he said, barely turning his head and acknowledging Rose and me.

"Not a problem," Rose said.

"A formality," the guy said and walked away.

Jerry shook his head when the man was out of sight but kept any thoughts to himself.

Inga appeared next at the doorway. "Henderson is in his cabin."

"Want to go get him? We can notify you if he calls us back," Jerry said.

"Sure," she said.

"We're just leaving, can we join you?" Rose said. Her request surprised me and from their expressions, the other two.

Inga glanced at Jerry, and he nodded his head.

"Sure," she said again.

Once out among the passengers, Rose said, "Inga, I want to help Jerry and, I guess, the captain by writing a letter to the CEO of this cruise line. I think they might be getting in trouble for something that is not their fault. Would you mind getting me the address and name of the person or people I could contact who might be the best people to write in their defense."

"Yes, I will," Inga said without further comment.

Henderson had a cabin not far from Sarah's. An interesting coincidence, I thought. As we approached the room, one of the cabin stewards came out of an alcove and joined us.

"He and another guy, who has a room just over there," the steward said and pointed to one of the doors not far away, "went into his cabin when I called." The steward led us to Henderson's cabin.

Inga knocked. "Mr. Henderson, I'm with ship's security. May we come in and talk?"

No one responded from inside the room, but I thought I heard some murmuring and movement from inside.

"Open the door," Inga instructed the steward.

I could see Rose tense up, and I shared her concern. If either Henderson or his associate was the murderer, we could use some reinforcements, but the steward and Inga went into the room like they expected nothing. Without a doubt our law enforcement backgrounds caused Rose's and my apprehension, while their service industry background resulted in their lack of concern.

I remembered too many things that went wrong for me or others when pursuing routine leads and responding to supposed non-violent incidents. Cops get shot at routine traffic stops, or they get knifed when they stumble into noisy family arguments or street corner drug deals. You learn to anticipate the worst, but despite my concerns, I followed the two into the room and Rose came in right behind me.

The two men inside had already gone into panic mode. One man was opening the sliding glass door to the balcony and shouted, "Here!"

He held his hands out ready to catch something. His friend was trying to unravel a shoe box from a wad of clothing that had been wrapped around it. "Throw it!" the man by the balcony shouted.

"Stop!" Inga ordered, but the men ignored her.

The man got the box untangled and tossed it, but his bad aim or shaky nerves caused the box to fly to the other man's left. He tried to make a one handed catch but the box ricocheted off his hand to the floor.

Rose leapt onto and over the bed, but the man had no intention of letting her get it. I jumped to her defense, pulling the man away from her and shoving him back. If I had some hope that everything would then calm down, I was sadly mistaken. The man pulled a steak knife out of somewhere and charged me with the knife stretched out in front and streaking toward my face.

All I could do in a situation like that was react, and with no room to maneuver, fleeing was not a choice. I grabbed the wrist of his knife hand with both my hands, twisted my body and pulled him toward me and down. My idea to place him in some sort of arm bar or arm lock might have worked if I had more space. As it was, we both tumbled on the bed in an uncomfortable, tangled mess.

Luck and the few more pounds that I had put on than I had meant to since my retirement came to good use, as I landed on top of him. He lay face down, and I still had my grip on his right wrist. I used my weight to help keep his right side pinned down while I kept his right arm and the knife from going anywhere.

Rose put a knee to the left side of his back and pressed a thumb behind his ear. "Let go of the knife, and we'll let go of you," she said.

"Bitch!" he screamed, but his remark only encouraged Rose to press in harder with her thumb. He let go of the knife, and I grabbed it.

"I got it," I said.

Rose backed away from him, and I carefully got off him and the bed. He didn't move. I looked over at Inga. She had a grip on the other man's arm, but he stood there next to her without offering any resistance. Inga said something on her phone before putting it back in her pocket.

"A full security team will be here in a minute," she said.

"I was just keeping it for him," the man in Inga's grip said. "I didn't bring it on board."

"Shut up," the man on the bed ordered.

I held up the knife for Inga to see.

She looked at the knife and said, "Hang onto it until the team gets here."

Rose closed the glass door to the balcony. "I'm going to pick up the shoebox and whatever is inside now. Jim, if he makes any move toward me, will you stab him in the leg."

"With pleasure," I said and moved closer to him. He must have realized that with the balcony door closed, the odds of his getting to the box first and getting rid of it, before the two of us stopped him and possibly stabbed him, were pretty low.

"Bitch," he grunted, but he didn't move.

Rose retrieved the shoe box and took it to Inga. She repeated her instructions to Rose, "Hold onto to it until the team gets here."

"What's in it?" Rose asked the man in Inga's grip.

The man first looked at his associate. I looked too and only saw anger and frustration in the face of the man on the bed.

"I'm not sure. He called it juice. I think it's a steroid, and he said it wasn't illegal in Mexico," the man next to Inga said.

"Are you Henderson?" Inga asked, and the man next to her nodded. "And you? What's your name?" The man on the bed didn't answer.

"You know, you are really stupid," I said. "It will only take them about five minutes to identify you."

"I've broken no laws. You can't do anything to me. You broke into his cabin and attacked us. I think I might sue."

"Should I throw him overboard?" I tried to keep a straight face.

"Too many witnesses, we can always do it later," Inga said. She kept her voice flat with no emotion.

Both men's eyes widened.

"Here they come," the steward said. He had positioned himself in the doorway, and waved at the approaching group. The steward stepped aside, and Johann Needles came into the cabin.

"Everything under control?" he asked.

"It is now, sir," Inga said. "We had to subdue the gentleman on the bed. He had an urgent desire to throw this overboard." Rose held the shoebox up in front of her.

"What's in it?" Needles asked.

"Drugs, apparently," Rose said. "We haven't opened it. The lid is taped down. Must be important to him," she nodded toward the man on the bed, "since he attacked Jim with a steak knife in an effort to get it from us."

Needles mumbled something about the whole world going to hell before he stepped aside and instructed one of his men to restrain the man on the bed.

"Jim, why don't you and I step out of the room, so we won't be in the way," Rose said.

Inga, Rose, and I stepped out of the room and four security personnel moved in. Inga brought Henderson out with her. "Do we have to restrain you?"

"No," Henderson replied. "I screwed up by telling him he could keep his box in my room until we got back, but that's all I'm guilty of. I won't cause you any problems. He said they weren't illegal in Mexico."

"We heard you the first time," Inga said.

Two men from Needles' team brought the man out of the

room. They had secured his hands behind his back with plastic flexi cuffs.

"You put them on too tight," the man snarled, but no one seemed to care.

"Inga," Needles called from inside the room. She went inside, and the rest of us waited in the hall.

For the first time, I noticed about a dozen passengers in the hallway watching us. I felt like shouting the show's over, but I knew it wasn't my show to control.

Needles came out of the room and shut the door behind him. He looked around before speaking. "Inga and two of my team will stay here and search the room. The rest of us will head back, but before we go, Esteban, take the knife as evidence from Mr. West. Deputy Luna, bring the box with you, please." He started walking away from the room, and the rest of us followed.

The rest of us included our two prisoners, Rose, the original steward who went into the room with us, two of Needles' team, and me. We made up quite the gaggle. I watched Henderson as he walked freely among us. I wondered if he was thinking about running, but where would he go?

I put my arm around Rose and squeezed her shoulders before letting go. "Are you ok?" I whispered.

"Yes, and you?" she said.

"I might be dreaming about that knife in my face for a few nights, but I'm fine."

We all crowded into one elevator and descended. In the elevator, I noticed a tear coming out of Henderson's right eye. He quickly brushed it with the back of his left hand. I imagined being trapped in the small space of an elevator and descending to somewhere unknown reinforced his sensation of despair.

I felt his concern wasn't warranted, but he hadn't been through this before. I felt like telling him to be honest, and things wouldn't turn out too bad for him, but I stayed quiet, and he discovered that on his own. An hour later, he left to go back to his cabin unescorted.

"Well, that was interesting," Jerry said to me after Needles had finished the interview and Henderson left. "A successful drug seizure and a confession by the accomplice, normally that would be enough for a good day. However, we're no closer to our murderer, and I feel like we just wasted a couple of hours."

"At least we cleared Henderson of the murders," I said.

"A couple things we still need to double check, but I agree with you. I don't see him as our killer," Jerry said.

"What's going to happen to him?" Rose asked.

"He'll be confined to his cabin and most likely banned from any future cruises with us. His buddy will remain in confinement and turned over to U.S. authorities along with the contents of the box. He will also be banned."

"Too bad he probably won't serve any jail time," Rose said.

"Maybe he would, if he had just stabbed Jim," Jerry said and tried to keep a straight face.

"Yes, that would have been better," Rose said.

"Thanks," I said.

Chapter 30

Rose and I had missed lunch and decided to remedy that by heading straight toward a hotdog stand I'd wanted to check out since seeing it the first day of the cruise. The small counter offered a few more choices than hot dogs, but they didn't deter me from my target. I ordered two hotdogs and French fries, and Rose settled for a coke and half my fries.

"So you think the knife in your face will bother your sleep tonight?" she asked once we were settled at a small table.

"Probably," I said and created a small mountain of ketchup next to the fries.

Rose quickly separated a portion of the fries, placing them as far as she could on the plate away from the ketchup.

"I'll have to see if I can keep your mind off any bad thoughts tonight," she said.

"It was a scary knife, it might take a lot of effort," I said and created a barrier with a few fries to help prevent the ketchup from spreading toward her fries.

"Ha! Don't push your luck," she said. "I know PTSD is real, but I also think we as a species have evolved with widespread PTSD a normal part of that evolution. We have it pretty good now, but I can't imagine living in the past or even in some countries today where life is cheap, and those with power take whatever they want."

I didn't know where she was going with her comments. There were a number of things I still remember that haunt me. None of which I would classify as PTSD, but someone else might. The mind captures and stores data in a peculiar way.

I can remember fights I got into as a kid but nothing else about the days before or after the fight. I can't remember much that happened during the fight day except for being in the fight and a few related things. I can see the ring of kids around us. Yes, there was an actual ring of kids around us watching. Of course, that's because we "called each other out" during school, so word got around. My other few fights happened without much warning, so there was no audience.

"Don't get me wrong," Rose said. "I'm all for the care and concern that we provide victims. It's just from my view point, very few people get to live a life free of a qualifying PTSD incident, and if you go back in time, life could really suck. Who we are today is a result of whole generations of PTSD affected people."

"I can see your point, being a cave man was not an easy life."

"Alright, make fun of me."

"No, I don't mean it that way," I said. "In fact, I agree with you. I really do. There's no bounds to man's cruelty, and you don't have to look far to see it."

"It's more than just that. When I was little, I watched a good friend lose part of her leg after a snake bite. I was there when she got bit, went with her to the hospital, and saw her days later after they had to remove part of her leg. I still dream about that now and then. That happened when I was ten."

I didn't think that compared to a soldier in World War I being on the receiving end of repeated artillery and gas attacks and then being told to charge the enemy a few times. At some point, that has to affect you, no matter who you are. However, I also thought that my idea proved her point. Even our soldiers have it better today than the soldiers back then.

"How is she doing now?" I asked.

"I haven't had any contact with her since high school. Her family moved before her senior year."

I took my last bite of hot dog and considered going back for another. Free food does that to you. Rose stood up and walked over to the hot dog man. A moment later she returned with a hot dog that had been cut in two.

"I'll split it with you," she said, reinforcing my opinion that she was a keeper.

A family with four children between the stages of toddler and teenager arrived and noisily invaded our space. Both parents looked worn out, and it didn't get any better when one of the children squirted her brother with ketchup.

Rose and I finished our hotdog and left.

"So, really, what do you think of Inga?" she asked.

"Who?" I asked. I had to smile when she slapped my arm. "Oh, that Inga."

"Like you'd forget," she said.

"Fairly attractive, but all business, wouldn't you say?"

"I think she's beautiful. They should use her on a magazine or television ad, and your saying that she is all business is kind of sexist. She is trying to do her job. You wouldn't say that about a guy."

"I would, too," I said.

"You're trying to get her to smile and to warm up to you," Rose said.

"Is that bad?"

"No, not at all, but don't say she's all business when she doesn't respond immediately to your charms," she said.

"What's going on here?"

"The cruise gets over tomorrow. We've been a little preoccupied, I'd say, with this investigation. I want to get to know you better before I make the decision to meet Chubbs or not. As you said, it's a big step for a guy to take a girl home to meet his dog."

"So, straight to the third degree," I said.

"No bright light in the face or uncomfortable hard chair, but yes, I guess I'm starting to get a little anxious."

I took her hand in mine, but didn't know what to say.

"Are you?" she asked.

"Of course," I said. I knew I should say something more but wasn't sure what was the right thing to say. When she let go of my hand and walked over to the rail, I knew not saying something might have been worse than saying something dumb.

She looked out over the water. "It's beautiful," she said.

"It is," I said and put my arm around her shoulders.

Chapter 31

Ed moved from one corner in the ship's library to the other, keeping his back to the door. He also took his hat off. Someone walking by outside might not think he was the same person. He looked at his watch, and calculated the hours left on the cruise. Only eighteen left. He wondered if he could sneak back to his cabin, or if the nosy cabin steward might be hanging around.

He had already made up his mind that if they sent someone to escort him to the security offices again to be interviewed, he wouldn't struggle with them. He would portray pure innocence and a little confusion. He had taken precautions and worn a disguise on both murder outings. "Murder outings," what a novel way to look at them, he smiled and looked around the library.

Ed felt more like himself. Since early morning he had not felt the presence of the other "thing" trying to control his mind.

"Just keep calm," he said softly. The Wind had to be a creation of his own imagination. Maybe stress brought it about. He stood up and stretched before heading out into the bright sun and fresh air. Only a few people were milling about, and he wondered if the news about the murders had people afraid. In a strange way, the thought made him smile.

He saw another ship in the distance travelling in the opposite direction and wondered if the ships travelled in specified shipping lanes. It made sense he thought, but with today's satellite technology and the vastness of the seas, he wondered if shipping lanes were simply an old fashioned habit. If he made it off this ship, maybe he would look into getting a job with one of the major cruise lines. Certainly, they could use an experienced accountant.

Rather than head to his cabin, Ed found himself returning to the upper deck in the front of the ship where he had hidden right after listening to the phone message that morning. Two couples were sunbathing on the reclining lounge chairs that they had adjusted all the way back to the horizontal position. Staying away from the sunbathers, Ed sat down on one of the lounge chairs next to the side wall. The wall protected him from the steady breeze and allowed the sun to heat him to a sweat in a few minutes. He closed his eyes and let the sun to do its thing.

A nearby voice startled him. He opened his eyes, only to have them blinded by the bright sun. He must have dozed for a few minutes. Shading his eyes, he looked around and saw one of the crew wait staff talking to the four sun bathers. Another member of the crew rearranged a couple of lounge chairs that had been pushed into a corner. Ed stood up and had to grab the railing next to him to maintain his balance. He took a few breaths to steady himself before leaving.

He hadn't gone far before his sense of relief shattered.

"Mr. Anderson? Mr. Henry Anderson?"

Ed turned his head and saw two members of the crew, both men, approaching him. One was studying a photograph. Ed froze and a voice in his head told him to relax.

"That is you, isn't it? Henry Anderson?" the older of the two men asked. He looked European. His partner, on the other hand, was definitely from Asia.

"Yes," Ed answered and raised his eyebrows, hoping the two

men would take the expression as one of innocent bewilderment.

"Mr. Anderson, will you come with us? The captain has a few questions," the older one asked.

"Of course, but may I use the restroom first. I was heading there just now." At least that was true, and the restroom was right in front of them.

"Yes, we'll wait for you out here," the older one said.

Inside the restroom, Ed entered a stall, removing the knife from his pocket and placing it on the floor behind the toilet. It wouldn't do him any good to be discovered carrying the knife around.

"Lead on," Ed said, after he exited the restroom. He tried to stay calm, but he didn't like the way one of the men walked in front of him, and the other remained a couple steps behind him. They couldn't have discovered anything, since he had left no evidence, but what did they want?

They led him down to the lower decks to where he had been interviewed before. Unlike then, the rooms were crowded with people and something was going on. They didn't take him to an interview room like they had last time. Instead, they left him in a break room.

"Please wait here. Things are a little busy right now," his escort said and left him.

A member of the cruise staff stood next to a long side table and poured coffee into a cup. After taking a sip and apparently satisfied, the crew member left without saying a word to him.

Ed heard yelling come from down the hall. The noise didn't help his nerves, but he stood up and moved closer to the door, hoping he might hear something that could help. Nothing did until a nearby door open, and he heard two men talking.

"Thanks again, Mr. Anderson, for coming in. Sorry to have bothered you," a voice in the hall said.

"That's alright," said a second voice. Mr. Anderson, Ed thought. "You sure you can't tell me what this is all about?"

"No, please don't concern yourself, we are simply following up on a few things," the first voice said again.

They said their goodbyes, and the hall became quiet. Even the yelling that had come from farther away than the next room had stopped.

It couldn't be a coincidence, Ed thought. They were interviewing people with the last name of Anderson. That made no sense to him, but he was sure he heard the name correctly. He moved away from the door moments before a young man in ship's uniform opened the door.

"Mr. Anderson, please come with me," the man said.

Ed followed him to a nearby room, where the man left him alone again. Ed sat in a chair next to a desk. Other than standing, the only other option would have been to sit in the chair behind the desk.

"Mr. Anderson, how are you doing today?" Johann Needles said as he walked into the room. He extended his hand, and Ed stood up and shook hands.

"Why have you brought me down here?" Ed asked while his mind started spinning.

"Just routine," Needles said. "Trying to close the loop on everything before we dock and everyone gets off the ship tomorrow."

Ed felt his mouth drying up. "Okay," he said.

Relax, don't volunteer anything, the voice in his head whispered.

"The information we have on you in our files seems to be missing a few things," Needles said.

"What do you mean?"

"It's rather embarrassing, but we had a data glitch, and we're just trying to fix a couple things before we reach Galveston. Could you give me your home address again?"

"My home address?"

"Yes, please. We only need a few pieces of information."

Ed gave him his Montclair, New Jersey address.

"Your employer?" Johann asked.

"My employer?" Ed asked. His mind flashed warning signs. They're trying to make a connection, but if they already knew where Joe Lassiter worked they should know about him, too. Except he didn't work there anymore, he wouldn't be on the company's roster.

"Yes, please," Johann said.

He mentioned the small accounting firm for which he had done a few temporary jobs since leaving Hudson Financial Data Management.

"Have you ever been employed by Hudson Financial?"

"No, I haven't."

"Did you ever know a Joe Lassiter?"

Ed had anticipated this and did his best to stay calm. "No, I don't believe so? Why are you asking me all this?"

"Just routine," Johann said. He asked Ed a few other questions about his past, but Ed was prepared for them and kept his responses in line with his cover story. After a minute, Needles wrote something down and stood up. "Would you mind staying here for another minute or two? I need to check on something and will be right back." He turned and left the room without waiting for a response.

What was going on, Ed wondered, and then it hit him: the other Anderson. They were looking for the right Anderson. They must have talked to people at the company and somehow linked Lassiter to him. He hadn't expected them to be so quick, but why didn't they know he was the Anderson they were looking for?

The door to the room opened and an attractive woman peered into the room. "Ed?" she said.

He almost acknowledged her when it hit him: the name. No one on the ship knew him as Ed, and anyone who would have mentioned him from the company knew him only as Ed. He hadn't ever gone by his first name, and even his middle name had been shortened to Ed or Eddy as a child. Named at birth Henry Theodore Anderson to appease both grandfathers, his mother called him Teddy or Teddy Bear until he was old enough to protest. Since then, he was Eddy and then Ed.

Ed smiled at the woman. "Sorry, not me, my name is Henry."

The woman left and a minute later, Needles reappeared. "Thanks for coming in, Mr. Anderson. You're free to go."

"Thanks," Ed said and left.

He walked out of the staff only area and past the reception counter. Suddenly, the man who had seen him talking to himself by the coffee station the night before came into view. Ed turned to his right and finding a brochure on a small table, picked it up and pretended to study it. The man from the night before walked past him but stopped a few feet in front of the reception counter. Ed took a furtive glance at him. The man had his back to him. He tried to listen to what he and the two women he was with might be talking about, but the room was too loud with all the people mingling nearby.

Ed wanted to walk away, but the women had caught his attention. The tall blond wore a ship's uniform and was beautiful. The shorter, dark haired one next to her was attractive, but the blond overshadowed her.

"She might be worth the risk," a voice said. He almost answered it, when he realized the voice had come from within his mind. Ed walked away from them and took the stairs up a deck. He found a spot where he could watch the deck below through the circular open space that ran from the fourth deck to the top of the ship. Not wanting to be too obvious, Ed backed away a few feet from the edge.

"Yeah, you're right. We can find someone like her once we're off the ship," the voice in his head said.

"You're not there. There is no we," Ed hissed and looked around to make sure no one was close enough to hear him.

"Don't be a fool. I'm here to stay, and you'll need me to get off the ship. I'm not only here, you named me. The Wind, ooooh, I like that name."

Ed shivered. He had hoped because he hadn't been bothered by this other persona since shortly after waking up, that it might have gone away. How stupid, he thought. Getting rid of this other creature in him wasn't going to be easy.

The Wind whispered in his mind, "That's right, it won't be easy. It might be easier for me to get rid of you, but if you just give me something now and then, like that blond we saw, I promise to stay away. At least until I get hungry again."

The dark haired woman and the man reappeared in the foyer below. Ed wondered who they were and what the man might have told the blond member of the crew.

Chapter 32

"I hope they don't send me a survey after this cruise," I said to Rose as we returned to our cabin.

"That would be funny," she said. "How would you rate the tranquility of your cruise? One for very relaxing on down to ten for being attacked by a mob hit man and almost stabbed by a drug smuggler."

"Somehow, I don't think they'll be sending out any surveys for this cruise. Might ruin the curve," I said.

"They'd be smart not to. Even for a passenger not touched by any of this, how would you rate a cruise with two murders and a missing person? Not to mention a drug bust and canceling one destination."

"I didn't even think of our skipping that last stop, but you're right. A lot of people will complain about that," I said, as we arrived at our cabin. "What say we hang the do not disturb sign on the door and stay in our room for the rest of the trip?"

"I'd love to, but we've agreed to help out, and we have to be prepared to talk to the authorities when we get to Galveston," Rose said.

"Ugh," I said.

"That's not a word." Rose took the sign from me and hung it on the outside door handle before closing the door. "And besides, I didn't say we couldn't leave it for an hour or so."

Unfortunately, the phone didn't give us an hour or so. We ignored the first call, but when the phone started ringing again, Rose answered it. After listening for a few seconds, she said,

"Okay, we'll be there shortly."

"Don't tell me," I said.

She returned to the bed and sat down next to me. "I think I'm going to ask for a refund," she said.

"What can they possibly want now?"

"Jerry just said something's come up. He told me to bring you with me."

"Who else would you bring?" I asked.

She smiled at that, "My loyal sidekick."

We both got dressed and left the room. In the elevator, we joined a family already heading to early dinner. Once we were off the elevator and alone, I said, "Let's hope they don't work us through dinner. The last night on the cruise is usually one of the better meals."

"We're not employees, Jim. We can break for dinner whenever we want to."

"I wonder when they close the dining room doors."

"We can always get a bite to eat somewhere on this ship," Rose said.

"Yes, but tonight, I wanted to have a nice dinner with you in the dining room."

"Sweet," she said and grabbed my hand to hold for a few seconds.

Jerry met us when we reached the reception area and led us back to his office. Johann Needles, Inga, and another crewman, whom I had not met, were there waiting for us.

"We've had a classic example of where the right hand didn't know what the left hand was doing. But first, take a look at this picture." He handed Rose a four by six-inch piece of paper with a picture of a man's face on it.

"It could be our guy in the picture," Rose said and handed it to me.

"That's the guy I saw last night talking to himself," I said.

"What?" Jerry said.

"He was sitting alone up by the coffee station on deck ten or eleven and arguing with himself. Spooked me a little, but I didn't think too much about it until he walked away. His gait made me think of the guy in the security video."

"Hardly conclusive, but it's interesting, considering he is also the man with whom the missing woman left the bar," Jerry said.

"You mean Sofi, the one we think the mob guy may have killed?" Rose asked.

"Yes," Jerry said.

"But why or how did you grab this picture of him?" I asked.

"Oh, yes, I got ahead of myself. He's our third Mister Anderson," Jerry said.

"That's too many coincidences," I said. "You need to get him in here."

"We had him here not all that long ago," Jerry said.

"I don't mean to be out of place, but why did you let him go?" Rose asked.

"Like I said, we screwed up. My guy, the one who first interviewed Anderson and searched his room as part of our search for Sofi, was assigned shortly thereafter to be our liaison with the security team that arrived yesterday. In his defense, at that time we had too many reasons not to think Anderson was involved in the other killings or with the missing woman. The worst part was that his name was never put in any file, because my guy had been given what seemed at the time a higher priority, and he put off documenting the interview of Anderson until later."

"We understand, it's not like those things haven't happened to all of us," I said.

"What reasons did you have to think Anderson wasn't our man?" Rose said.

"He doesn't wear glasses and has a moustache. Basic disguise techniques, I know. He was also in the Sky Lounge around the time of Lassiter's murder," Jerry said.

"Around the time?" I said.

"Yes, we did a cursory check and verified it, but we've looked again, and the first purchase he made came about ten minutes after he claimed he got there," Jerry said.

"So, it is possible he has no alibi?" Rose said.

"Right, we only caught it today when one of the team that searched his room saw him leaving our offices. He asked someone else what was going on, and then the two of them went to Johann."

"Well, it's too many coincidences for me," I said. "You need to get him back in here and keep him until we reach shore."

"You need to call Agnes back," Rose said. "Maybe you should do it now."

I dialed her number, and the call went directly into voice mail. No answer. "We could call the other lady." I said, referring to Lassiter's personal assistant, or secretary, or whatever her title was.

"We'll have to get with Sarah to get her number," Rose said. "By the way, do you still have someone watching her door?"

"Yes," Jerry said, "and I'll make sure we keep someone there and with her while she departs the ship tomorrow."

"Good idea," I said.

"Jim, about this man last night," Inga said, "did you hear

what he was saying?"

"Not very well, and I had no idea who or what he was talking to or about. He was arguing."

"All along we've been thinking this guy may just be crazy," Inga said, looking at Jerry. "This Anderson character may check off that block, too."

"Another reason to get him back in here," Jerry said. "We have someone watching his room. We're hoping he's thinking he has fooled us, which shouldn't be hard for him because at the time he did."

"Can you change the lock code to his door?" Rose asked.

"Yes, we thought about that, but we're thinking it might be better to have him go into his cabin and then go get him. Keeping him out may simply spook him," Jerry said.

"What advice do the visiting experts have about this?" I asked.

"To be honest, we haven't told them. In addition to going over all the steps we have already taken, they are now busy going over the records for all the required training we're supposed to have done since our last inspection," Jerry said.

"They did come up with a list of suggestions for us to follow up on, but most of those were the same ones we had already done or were doing. They also did a final review of the crime scenes, but as we know that didn't give us anything. But now, I think they are just documenting evidence to further support what we all anticipate," Needles said.

"It sucks," Inga said.

"None of this will touch you," Jerry said, and Needles nodded in agreement.

"That's not the point, we do most of the training, and what we don't do physically, we require the crew do online. A lot of it is just understanding the policies, and we're not doing anything different than every other ship," Jerry said.

"Hey, let's focus on this guy Anderson. We get him, and things may not end too badly," Rose said.

Inga looked at Jerry who nodded back at her.

"What do you want us to do?" I asked.

"Confirming he was the guy you saw last night was one thing. Calling and getting Anderson's full name is another. We also want you to be with us for the interview and when we turn him over to the US authorities," Jerry said.

"What about the jurisdictional issues?" Rose asked.

"To be resolved, but an agreement has been made for our killer to be temporarily confined in Galveston pending extradition or whatever. The cruise must go on," Jerry said.

"Do you want us to wait here?" Rose asked Jerry.

"No, but we need you to tell us Anderson's full name once you get it, and come again when we call."

"We might be in the dining room," I said.

"Okay, why don't you two take off and go there now. It may get busy later," Jerry said.

"I think we've got him," I said to Rose, after we left them and walked to the dining room.

"I hope so. It's still a long way from locked in, but if this is the Anderson who got fired when Lassiter was hired, I think he is our killer. And, I think he may have killed the missing woman to add more confusion and stress on the investigation. He may, in fact, be insane," Rose said.

"But we have no evidence, and in the case of the missing woman, no body. Add that to the jurisdictional issues and short time left, getting to a successful prosecution may be impossible."

"The stress may get him to confess, or he may panic and make a mistake. Unfortunately, that mistake might include killing someone else," Rose said.

"I hope it doesn't get to that."

"I can't believe they had him and didn't connect him to the missing woman. When we gave them the name Anderson, they should've realized the connection."

"I agree, but I've seen a lot of screw ups in my life," I said. "A witness gave a friend of mine a license plate number of a vehicle seen leaving the scene of a burglary. It was a vanity tag, easy to remember. My friend, Vern, didn't make many mistakes, but on the way back to the office, he got called to respond to a barracks fight, something we didn't usually get involved with. In this one, though, a guy got stabbed. Well, my friend totally forgot about the license plate number until the next day. We found out later that if we had followed up on the tag the day before, we might have caught the guy, because the suspect didn't flee the area until the morning after Vern got the tag number."

"We all have stories like that. When I was a rookie, we had a crime photographer who, after leaving a homicide, had his camera stolen. He stopped at a Taco Bell and went inside because the drive through was all backed up. Left the camera on the front seat. He said he was only inside for a few minutes, but when he returned to his car, the window had been smashed and the camera was gone."

"It happens," I said. "They should find Anderson without too much of a hassle. I mean, where can he go?"

"He won't be able to get off the ship without being noticed either," Rose said.

"That's true," I said.

We arrived in the dining room right before they closed the doors. The dining room looked full, but the wait staff sat us at a table for eight that only had four other people at it.

"I guess they gave away our regular table," Rose whispered.

"At least we got in," I said.

The other two couples said hello, and we all exchanged names. They were travelling together and mentioned that the other four people with them had gone to a specialty restaurant for their evening meal.

"If you weren't so cheap, Fred, we could've gone, too," one of the women chastised her husband.

"This food is great, and it's already paid for. Why would we want to go elsewhere and pay for our meal?" Fred said.

His wife mumbled something back to him I couldn't hear. From that point on, the four didn't include us in their conversation. Their dessert came while Rose and I ordered our dinner. Up until the foursome left, Rose and I kept our conversation to the meal choices and cooking. I discovered that she had a lot of experience cooking, and she discovered I didn't.

"Life goes on," Rose said.

"What do you mean?"

"We're nearly one hundred percent absorbed in the murders and the investigation, and that foursome didn't seem to even have a concern about it," she said.

"Well, that's probably a good thing," I said.

"It is. I just find it's good for me to remind myself that while my life is swamped dealing with dirt bags and crime, there is a world out there that has other priorities. I hope to have other priorities, too, someday."

"You will," I said.

Chapter 33

I enjoyed our dinner and believed Rose did, too. For the most part we didn't talk about the investigation or even the cruise. We talked about those serious topics friends and lovers often talk about: if you could live anywhere in the world, where would it be? If you won the lottery, what would you do with the money? If you could go back to your eighteenth birthday, but know everything you do today, would you do it?

We laughed at ourselves, which was something we hadn't done very often in the whole time we'd known each other. Most of the dining room had emptied out, and we were about to leave when Inga approached us.

"Do you mind if I join you for a cup of coffee?" she asked.

I would've said we're leaving, but Rose beat me to the punch. "Sit down, please join us," Rose said.

"I'm glad I found you two," she said. "A lot has started happening."

I stayed silent and let Rose respond. I wanted to say we were with them barely an hour earlier. I wanted to ask what more could we do. I guess I wanted them to leave us alone for the rest of the trip.

"Did you find him?" Rose asked.

"No. He has not returned to his cabin. We've locked him out."

"I thought you weren't going to do that?" Rose asked.

"That's part of the reason I'm here and not someone higher up," Inga said. "Things have gotten a little stressed."

"How so?" Rose asked.

"When the team from the home office was updated on everything, they got nasty and went to the skipper."

"So, the idea of their coming here to assist has gone out the window," I said.

"Yes," Inga said. "The captain has taken charge of everything, but I'm not sure it was his idea."

"And your visitors are whispering in his ear?" I said.

"Yes, Sinclair Mathison and his team, and there's more. You two are supposed to stay away from the investigation. Rose, you will be called back in when we dock tomorrow morning. Jim, I'm sorry, but you are out."

I smiled and wondered if she thought my smiling was being sarcastic rather than glad to be out.

"That's okay," Rose said. "I just feel sorry for Jerry and all of you. I can't tell you how many times our sheriff's office has been second guessed and criticized by another agency. It's unfair."

"It's easy to look back after the fact and criticize. Afterwards, one has the benefit of a lot more information," I said. "I think it was Mickey Mantle who said he never knew how easy baseball was until he retired and became a sports announcer."

Inga looked a little confused.

"Like Monday night quarterbacking," I said. That didn't seem to help.

"We know what you mean," Rose said. "I'll be available in the morning, and I'll keep Jim out of sight."

"Promises, promises," I said.

Rose smiled at Inga and gave me an exasperated look. "Good luck on finding Anderson sooner rather than later," Rose said.

"There's no way he's getting off this ship before we've had a chance to talk to him," Inga said.

"If you've shared his picture with all the crew you have out patrolling the ship, someone ought to spot him soon?" I said.

"We hope so," Inga said. "This cruise has been the most stressful one I've ever been on. I can't wait to get back on a normal one. It'll probably be boring."

"I imagine you haven't gotten a lot of sleep on this one," I said.

"No, and it doesn't look like I'll get much tonight or tomorrow."

"Is the first day of a new cruise usually busy for you?" Rose asked.

"Yes, but it's more than that. We have a lot of work ensuring everyone debarks without a problem, and that all luggage and cargo, if we have any, get off okay. Tomorrow we have the additional stuff with the homicides and missing person. It's going to be a mess. I'm glad I'm so low in grade that I'll be outside the bloodletting. At least, I hope so," Inga said.

"I imagine there may be a lot of press there to greet the ship, too," I said.

"Television, too," Inga said. "You know the widow works for a major news outlet."

"We know," I said.

"We aren't supposed to have any contact with the press. The company will have a spokesperson there, but who knows what the passengers will say. It's going to be a nightmare." Inga shook her head at the thought of this.

"You need to keep your head down and stay out of the infighting," Rose said. "Believe me, you don't do anyone any good by trying to get your opinion in, and doing so can get yourself caught up as being part of the problem."

"Maybe so, but I feel like I owe my loyalty to Jerry and Johann and the skipper, of course."

"You do, but do it silently and behind the scenes. Write a letter to the company CEO and express your thoughts, but keep any emotions out of it," Rose said.

"Maybe I will. Johann has told me and the others not to get involved either, but I feel so bad. They haven't done anything wrong," Inga said.

"He gave you good advice," I said.

Inga nodded like she understood, but her eyes didn't share her conviction. "Thanks for having coffee with me. I better get back. Rose, we'll call you when it's time to come down, and Jim, if I don't see you again, it was nice to meet you."

We said goodbye and watched her walk away.

"She's a good kid. I hope everything turns out okay for her," I said.

"Even if she doesn't get hurt by all this, I imagine her love of cruising may take a hit, and if they come down too hard on her bosses, she may quit," Rose said.

"That's too bad."

"I wonder why Agnes never called you back?"

"Could be anything," I said. "She may have had second thoughts about talking to anyone on the phone that she doesn't know. Her boss at the company may have told her to not talk to anyone but the police."

"That's possible, especially if the press has been around there snooping, too."

"Let's stop by Sarah's room and update her. She needs to know what's going on, since we'll be in Galveston tomorrow morning."

"Guess we should," Rose said. "Lead on."

Two crew personnel sat outside Sarah's cabin, one male and one female. They both watched us approach.

"Hi," Rose said, "we're friends with Sarah Lassiter and would like to talk to her."

They both stood and looked at us suspiciously, but the man knocked on the door. Sarah opened the door and seeing us ushered us in.

"Rose, I hope you feel better today than I do," Sarah said. "I had quite the hangover. You would think I'd know better than try to drink with my cousin by now."

"It took me a while to get going this morning," Rose said.

"If you're here to try to get me out for dinner, I've already eaten. I plan on staying in here until we dock."

"No, we're not here to take you anywhere," I said. "We think we know who the killer is, Sarah. The crew is looking for him now."

"What? Who?"

"A guy named Anderson. We think he was fired to make room for Joe, when he was hired at his new job," I said.

"You don't kill someone for that," Sarah said.

"There may be more to it," Rose said, "but we need to talk to him to find out everything. That is if he will even talk to us."

"Do they think he killed the crewman, too?" Sarah asked.

"Yes, he also looks similar to the man in the security footage, and," Rose said and looked at me for a second, "we think he may be a little bit insane."

"What?"

"I think by chance I sat close to him last night when I left you all here. I stopped at a coffee kiosk up on the deck. One other person was there, Anderson. He was sitting off to the side arguing with himself," I said.

"He didn't have one of those Bluetooth things?" Sarah said.

"No, I didn't see one."

"Why didn't they grab him last night?"

"There was a little screw up. They actually had him in to talk to this afternoon. Only after they let him go did someone point out he was the last person whom we know the missing woman was with," Rose said.

"The missing woman?"

"I think we mentioned it to you," Rose said.

"I remember something about it, but I didn't think it was related to Joe. Why would it be? I don't understand," Sarah said.

"That's what has made this whole thing so difficult. None of it relates, except for the murder weapon with Joe and the crewman," I said. "The fact that the missing woman's traveling partner turned out to be aggressive and violent encouraged everyone to think that her disappearance could be handled as a separate matter."

"The main thing now, though, is that if we can connect Anderson with two murders, and we can put the missing woman with him as the last person to see her alive, we have more of a reason to think he might have been involved with her disappearance," Rose said.

"Seems all like a stretch to me," Sarah said.

"I agree," Rose said. "With what we have now, even a bad defense attorney could get the whole thing thrown out."

"But, there is a lot of circumstantial evidence," I said. "They can't ignore it. We have a motive, even if it is a weak one. We have opportunity. While the security video we have is not good, what they have captured seems to be him."

"Seems?" Sarah asked and shook her head. "They'll need to get a confession or find the weapon with his prints on them."

"We're sure he tossed the weapon overboard," Rose said.

"Any prior record?" Sarah asked.

"Nothing at all," Rose said.

"I've gotten a number of messages from work. All have been expressions of condolences, but more than a few have hinted for a story. I've ignored them. I don't have any interest in writing about all this. Maybe if they got a confession, and I knew why someone would kill Joe, writing about it might be therapeutic, but otherwise I'm just too upset and confused," Sarah said.

"Are you going to need any help packing or getting ready for tomorrow?

"Thanks, Rose, but my cousin will be here first thing in the morning. Someone from the crew will also be here to help."

"I imagine the cruise line would prefer getting you off the ship and away from any press that I'm sure will be there to meet us," I said.

Sarah nodded. "Ironic, if this happened to someone else, and I wasn't on this cruise, I might be one of those in the press waiting for a story out there with them."

"Do you know if Joe's parents will be out there?" I asked.

"I've gotten mixed signals. They were in shock when they heard the news, as were all of us. I didn't get a firm answer, and they haven't called me back since the one phone call. You know, Joe and I were going to rent a car and go to San Antonio next. He always wanted to see the Alamo. We weren't flying back for another three days."

"Have you made reservations to get back to New York?" Rose asked.

"Not yet, I plan on spending tomorrow in Galveston. I mean, I don't know what I'll have to do, or whom I'll have to talk to about everything."

"Will anyone be staying with you?" Rose asked.

"My cousin," Sarah said.

"Good," I said. "Rose and I will be sticking around for a while, too. She has to be involved with the exchange of information and whatever with the local police and any federal authorities that get involved."

"Well, I don't have to, but I said I would," Rose said. "Can we stay in touch with you? We may be spending the night in Galveston, too."

"Of course," Sarah said. "This has all been too much for me. Too many emotions. First was disbelief, then sadness. Then I became angry this happened and afraid for myself. Next, I wanted to run away and pretend none of this happened. Now, I'm nervous and dreading tomorrow. I mean I'm glad they may have caught the murderer, but it really doesn't make me feel any different. He's ruined my life."

I wondered about that last statement. I had the impression that the first thirty hours of her marriage hadn't been all bliss. Maybe for some childish reason I had exaggerated Joe's shortcomings, but still I thought her statement about her life being ruined was an exaggeration.

"It will take time," Rose said.

Someone knocked on the cabin door, and Sarah's head jerked toward it. "Excuse me. That startled me for some reason." She stood up and went to the door. "Oh, yes, come on in."

Sarah led a member of the crew into the room. Despite all my trips to the ship's offices, I hadn't seen the woman before. She looked to be about my age with a touch of grey in her brown hair. She wore enough bars on her shoulder boards to indicate she was one of the higher ranking officers on the ship. She carried a clipboard with a number of forms on it.

"As you can imagine, I have a lot of paperwork to fill out," Sarah said to us.

"Do you need us to stay?" Rose asked.

"No, I don't think so," Sarah said and looked at the crew person.

"There's nothing here that accuses you of anything at all or has you signing away any of your rights. I'm Barbara Brian, chief of administration and personnel. I'm very sorry for what happened. These papers are advisory in nature, provided for your information, and are required by our legal department."

"I can handle this alone," Sarah said.

"Ok, we'll stay in touch," Rose said.

We left them alone. "Should we get one final ice cream treat?" I asked.

"You can't be hungry. We'll just get one, and I'll share," she said.

Chapter 34

Ed got off the elevator and had started down his hallway when he spotted two crew personnel standing by his door. He made an abrupt u-turn, hoping they hadn't noticed him. Instinctively, he started thinking about places where he could hide for a while. If he could stay out of sight until it was time to disembark.

"You need more of a plan than hiding," the voice in his mind said.

"Go away, I don't need you," Ed said out loud. He looked around to make sure no one could hear him.

The Wind spoke to him again, "The bathroom where you hid the knife. No one will bother you there."

Ed wanted to yell in frustration, but he realized that the bathroom might be an excellent place to hide. It was out on a secluded part of the deck and most people would be inside now that it was dark. Besides, he wondered if he might need the knife again.

He reached the bathroom without encountering any of the crew, and as expected, it was empty. He went into the stall in which he had hidden the knife and closed the door. After retrieving the knife, he sat down on the toilet. It wouldn't be the most comfortable place to hide, but it might work.

"Now for the plan," The Wind spoke in his mind again.

This time Ed decided to listen. Maybe he did need a plan.

"There may be no way to get off this ship without being detained again. We need to get ahead of them."

"What do you mean," Ed said.

"Easy, once we're in American waters and close to shore, call an attorney, get represented. When they stop us from leaving, and they will, we refuse to answer anyone's questions about anything. Tell everyone you're being used as a scapegoat because of the crew's incompetence in solving the woman's disappearance. Tell your lawyer you know nothing at all about any murders."

Ed liked this idea and wondered if it might work.

"Of course it will work," The Wind said.

For a brief moment, Ed wondered how The Wind knew what he was thinking.

"Ask the lawyer to get you off the ship immediately. Tell him you're terrified they will sail away with you still on board, and that you will lose all your rights. Tell him no one ever advised you of your rights for anything, that they've already searched your room and interviewed you twice. Tell the lawyer that he needs to ask them for any evidence that they have to indicate that you may have done anything wrong. They don't have anything."

"Yes," Ed said out loud. Any evidence that might be on the ship would sail away with it. He wondered how long he should wait before he went back to his room. He needed his passport that was in his room, and it would look more natural if he had his luggage with him, rather than try to sneak off the ship without any luggage. That would look suspicious.

"That's right," The Wind said. "We'll work this together and nothing will happen to us."

Ed had a desire to scream at this other persona that had taken up residence in his mind. How could this happen. What was it, this thing he named The Wind? Was it a bunch of faulty neurons, a chemical imbalance? How could something else invade his mind? No, not just invade, this thing had moved in like a squatter and wouldn't leave.

"Ha! Ha! A squatter, I love the way you deny reality. How about if we go back to the devil made me do it excuse," the voice in his mind said.

Ed leaned back and closed his eyes. He didn't have the desire to argue. With a little luck, in about twelve hours he would be off this ship. He could go to someplace like Alaska and never be found again.

As he started to fall asleep, the outer door to the restroom opened. Someone walked in and went to the urinal. Ed relaxed a little, and a minute later, the person left without washing his hands.

"Yuck," Ed said and made a mental note to use a paper towel when opening the door.

After a few minutes, he dozed off only to have his sleep interrupted by someone entering the restroom again. This time he could hear the sound of a bucket being pushed into the restroom.

"Sir, I need to clean and lock this restroom for the night. I'll be waiting outside," a man said in a voice with a strong accent.

"I'll be right out," Ed said. So much for a good hiding spot.

He left the restroom, keeping his head down, but he didn't see the crewman. He started walking and stayed out on the deck, keeping to the darker spots. He wondered if he could make it unnoticed down to deck four, or was it five, where he could try to hide in one of the lifeboats until morning. He had seen steel ladders attached to the sides of the ship that led up to catwalks that one could take to the lifeboats. Could he climb the ladders without being seen? If anyone spotted him, they would likely turn him in.

Ed looked out into the Gulf of Mexico and saw a series of lights in the distance. The off shore oil rigs, he thought. He had seen them when they left Galveston. They must be getting close, and he wondered if the ship was in cell phone range to make a call to a law office in Galveston. The thought didn't stay long in his mind as he remembered his cell phone was in his cabin. He hadn't purchased any of the Wi-Fi or phone options that were offered when he purchased his ticket.

"We need to find another place to hide."

"I know," Ed whispered, answering the other voice in his head.

"The safest place would be in someone else's cabin."

Ed thought about that. "How would we get into someone else's cabin without being noticed?"

"It would be easy. It didn't matter if someone was there, the only trick would be getting in, and I have an idea for that." The Wind's voice sounded soothing, almost hypnotic in Ed's mind.

"I don't want to hurt anyone else," Ed said.

"We also don't want to get caught either and spend the rest of our life in jail. What do you think, Ed? Would you like for the big boys to make you wear lipstick and silk panties? I could just fade away, but you would have to put up with it. You can't go anywhere. So, we really only have two choices."

"No, I don't want that to happen either," Ed said. "What if we go back to the cabin and let them arrest us if they want to?" Ed didn't realize he said we, but it hadn't gone unnoticed.

"Good question, Ed, but they won't let you sleep. They will interrogate you until they get you to slip up. They may even get physical in order to get a confession. You aren't on American soil, so you can forget about your constitutional rights. No, we've got to stay away until we can get a lawyer who can demand our immediate release. Once off the ship, we're scot free. You won't even need me anymore."

Ed considered his options, but knew he had only one. So far, the crew had treated him well, but all along he had also had the feeling they could do about anything they wanted to him. Visions of being tortured into confessing flooded his mind. He never considered that these images may have been the work of the other persona inside his mind fighting for control. In the end, he gave in.

"Okay, but how do we pick another cabin?" Ed asked.

"We might have to go shopping," The Wind said and shoved Ed further out of his own mind. He walked down to the section of the ship where the shops were located.

In the first souvenir shop he came to, Ed purchased a hat with a picture of a cruise ship on it, thinking peoples' eyes might be drawn to the hat rather than his face. He pulled it low over his forehead, before looking around for a potential target. Ed sensed that he had become less in control of his own actions, but this time he didn't fight the sensation. He knew getting off the ship had to be his first priority.

A young couple walked by him, the woman giggling at something her companion said. He let them pass and started to follow them as they left the shops, but the two walked straight into a nearby lounge.

Ed walked back into a jewelry store and pretended to be interested in a few items behind the thick glass counters. He eyed an older woman whom he estimated was in her mid-seventies.

She would be an easy target, he thought. The woman talked to the saleslady about a ruby and diamond necklace, while Ed feigned interest in the men's watches. Could she be rich? Ed wondered if there could be a boat load of cash in her room.

"Mona, come on, you know we can't afford anything else on this trip, and the kids want to play some games," a man said from the jewelry shop's doorway.

Ed assumed the man was the woman's husband, and behind him stood four other younger adults. The kids, Ed thought. After the woman left, Ed decided he had loitered long enough.

Chapter 35

Despite her protestations that she had eaten too much, Rose shared a banana split with me and ate her half without any complaints.

"That was good," Rose said. "My diet starts tomorrow, definitely."

"Not until after breakfast, I hope," I said. "We'll need our strength to fight the crowds getting off the ship."

"At least customs should be easy."

She didn't make eye contact with me, so I had no idea if that meant I was in trouble, or if she was kidding me. Was there some protocol about buying something expensive for one's lady friend during your first cruise?

Finally, she looked up, and her eyes and grin gave her away. "You're so easy. You really are an amateur when it comes to women. I didn't mean anything with my comment about customs, just giving you a hard time," she said and gave my hand a squeeze. "Come on let's get you back to the cabin." She stood up.

"One second," I said and walked back to the counter and ordered a cappuccino. "Want something?"

She shook her head no.

"Let's go out onto the deck for a few minutes while I drink this," I said.

"If you're trying to get me into the mood, I'm already there," Rose said.

"Want to go straight back?"

She laughed. "I'll last, besides you need to drink your cappuccino." She wrapped her arm around mine, and we strolled out of the shopping area.

At this moment, Ed left the jewelry shop and spotted a couple he recognized coming out of another corridor. The man was drinking a cup of coffee as he walked, and the dark haired lady next to him was rubbing a spot on her forehead. Even from this distance, maybe ten yards away from them, Ed could see a scar on her forehead that he hadn't noticed before. Ed instinctively stepped back out of sight.

This was the couple he had seen talking to the ship's officers. Hadn't he heard one of them, maybe the woman, being referred to as "deputy", and the man had been the one who witnessed him talking to himself. An idea swirled through Ed's mind.

"Too risky," Ed whispered and tried to control his thoughts.

"Risky, yes, but this could be perfect," the voice in his head replied. "If she's a cop and has been briefed on everything that the ship's security team knows, she may be trouble once we dock. Besides, she might be able to tell us what evidence the crew has discovered. Getting rid of both of them can only benefit us."

"We can't overpower both of them."

"Leave that to me," The Wind said, and Ed felt himself again fading even deeper into a haze. He fought to stay alert, but it felt like he dropped into a dream. He watched the couple walk farther away before he started following them. For reasons he didn't understand, the dread he had only moments before slowly changed to excitement.

The couple went out on deck, stopping outside the automatic sliding doors at the rail. They stared out into the darkness, and Ed, or the other entity that now controlled his mind, thought the couple must be talking about the lights that could be seen in the distance. Ed watched for a while before moving to a chair where he could see them, but he wouldn't be so obvious. Grabbing one of the flyers that were scattered on the various table tops, Ed pretended to be reading it.

The flyer contained information on disembarkation procedures along with information on how to book another cruise. When anyone walked by, he lowered his head, and the brim of the hat covered his face from any curious enough to look at him. He knew most had no interest in him.

Another couple sat across from him. They both held large martini glasses, and if he had to guess, they had been drinking for a while. The woman's martini had at least four olives in it, while the other had none. Although they kept shushing each other in a futile attempt to keep their conversation private, they both talked in that loud voice that often comes from drinking too much.

Ed tried to ignore them and keep his attention on the couple he was following, but the two out on the deck appeared in no hurry to go anywhere, and the inebriated couple across from him became more intriguing. The man's attempts to fondle the woman were met with half hearted defensive moves, and the woman's protestations focused more on his purchasing something he had promised for her, rather than any problems with the wide variety of things he proposed they should do once they get back to their cabin.

When the couple with the martinis left, Ed figured the woman had worked her companion up to such a state that the man would likely let her buy whatever she wanted to hurry up and get her back to their cabin.

Ed looked out for the couple on the deck and was surprised to see they were not there. He walked over to the doors that slid open as he approached them. He cautiously looked around, half expecting them to be only a few feet away, but they were walking towards the back of the ship. The man had his arm around the woman's shoulders, and she leaned against him.

"Good," he mumbled. The more distracted the better.

Other than the couple, no one else was out on the promenade. Maybe the darkness and knowledge of the murders kept most people inside. Ed thought about following the two but didn't want to become obvious or draw the man's curiosity. After all, the man might recognize him from the night before.

The couple stopped and leaned against the railing again. Rather than stay by the door, Ed moved to the rail and acted like he, too, had come out to enjoy the view. There wasn't much to see, but there was something captivating about watching the sea as the ship slid though it in the darkness.

He reached down by his side and felt the comfort of the knife.

Chapter 36

Out on deck, Rose and I leaned against the railing and watched the water churn and turn into waves that would form the ship's wake as it plowed through the Gulf. Enough light from the ship shown down onto the water near the ship to create a fascinating sight.

"It's almost mystical," Rose said.

"It is. I like it," I said. "I think if you stood here long enough, it could just about hypnotize you."

"Look out there," Rose said and pointed off toward some lights visible in the dark horizon. "Another ship?

"I think so, but it's pretty far away. They have some oil rigs in the Gulf, but I think that must be a ship."

We stood there in silence for a while before Rose suggested we walk a little and led me toward the stern of the ship. I thought she was taking me somewhere specific, but we stopped after a minute and leaned against the railing, looking out over the water.

"Jim," she said. "Where are we going in this relationship?"

This was worse than the Customs remark. I glanced at her, hoping to see some evidence of her trying to play me again and saw none.

"I'd like for it to continue, if that's what you mean," I said. Her cop training settled in, and she remained silent. The thought that the first one to speak loses went through my mind, but I was trapped. "If you're thinking that I might say thanks for a good time and then disappear after this cruise, you're very wrong."

"I've never thought that," she said but didn't volunteer more.

"If you're thinking about another cruise, I don't know. This one didn't turn out as expected," I said and quickly added, "the cruise, not us."

"I know what you mean, and I know I'm putting you on the spot, but I started thinking about us at dinner. I mean really thinking." She stopped talking and stared out into the darkness.

"I hope this isn't one of those 'It's not you, it's me' conversations," I said.

"I guess it kind of is. I enjoy being with you. I really do, and I want to continue seeing you. Maybe not on another cruise right away, but, you know, coming up to meet Chubbs, which by the way, might be a good nickname for you or me after this cruise."

"So?"

"You're making it hard on me."

Hard on her, I thought. How about me? I had no idea where this conversation was going when it started and still wasn't sure.

"I'm not sure what you want me to say, Rose. But if you want me to say that I'm in no hurry for you to make a commitment, consider it said. I really, really enjoy being with you. I want you to enjoy being with me."

"Good, say no more," Rose said and put a finger to my lips before following it with a kiss. "I want to see more of you, and maybe down the road something more may evolve out of our relationship. You know how much my life is messed up. I need to resolve a million things in my own mind, and I want to apologize for being so uptight all the time. I know I'm repeating myself, but I've had some bad experiences with the men in my life."

I felt a huge weight lifted off my shoulders but did my best to look sincere and understanding. I had dreaded how to handle the goodbyes that would come at the end of the cruise, and she had resolved it for me. Perhaps she thought I might have pressed her for some commitment. It made sense, and she had likely been as concerned about how I would handle our parting tomorrow as I was.

"It's my snoring, isn't it?" I said smiling.

"You don't want me to give you a list," she said and punched my arm.

"Still friends?"

It took her a few seconds to catch my joke. "No, I don't like you introducing me as a friend. I think the appropriate term these days is partner."

"You mean like a buddy? Howdy, partner," I tried to sound like the cowboys in the old western movies.

She smiled and shook her head. "Let's go back to the cabin. It's our last night, you know."

We turned away from the rail and started back the way we came. I noticed a man ahead of us in the shadows leave the railing. He disappeared inside, and as he did the hairs on the back of my neck started dancing. I reached back and rubbed my neck.

"Did you see that man?" I asked.

"The one that went inside?"

"Yes."

"Just that a man went inside. I didn't really see anything about him. Why? You getting jumpy?"

"I must be," I said.

We walked together making small talk, and once inside, I didn't see the man or anyone else that concerned me. The idea that something wasn't right, however, stayed with me.

Chapter 37

Ed, now completely under the influence of this other persona in him, had no problem finding a place to hide after he got inside. A group of seven, loud adults were walking towards the shops, and Ed hustled past them before slowing to their pace in hopes of looking like one of the group. He removed his baseball cap, and when the group stopped in front of the first shop, he did the same. They paid no attention to him, even as he looked through the group to watch the doors that led outside.

The man and woman he had been following came inside. The man looked around as though he was looking for something or someone, but Ed didn't think the man saw him. The two went to the elevators and after a short wait climbed into one.

As the doors shut, Ed put his hat back on and walked to the same set of elevators. He reached the elevators in time to watch the numbers that lit up above the elevator stop at eight. The other elevator doors next to him opened, and Ed jumped in, pushing the number eight.

He knew that there was a possibility that somebody else got on the elevator on eight, and that his couple continued up, but eight was his best bet. After all, what was that saying? Aces and eights, a dead man's hand, yes that was it, and he was the Ace. His elevator opened on the eighth deck, and Ed immediately saw the couple reaching for a door down the hall ahead of him and to his right.

He almost stayed inside the elevator for cover, but the doors started to shut. Rather than cause the elevator's alarm to sound or the doors rattle if he tried to stop them from shutting, Ed hurried out and moved behind a nearby wall. Peering around the edge of the wall, he watched the cabin door close behind the couple. He remained still for a few seconds, making certain he could find the right door when he went down the hall. All the alcoves and doors looked alike, and the last thing he wanted was to knock on the wrong door.

Ed had a simple and straight forward plan, yet the word "foolhardy" still drifted somewhere in the back of his mind. He would be going up against two people, but an overpowering confidence swept the concern away. He was once again The Wind, a proven, great assassin. Had anyone ever killed five people on a cruise ship and walked away a free man? He would be the subject of legends. Of course, the sea offered the perfect place to get rid of evidence, but why downplay the significance of what he would accomplish tonight.

An idea came to him that he should leave something behind to help the press refer to him as The Wind. That would be better than having them come up with some corny nickname on their own. Too late to worry about that now, he needed to concentrate on the task at hand.

The steak knife should be sufficient to do the job, he thought, and checked for it in his pocket before he started walking toward the door. He went through the possible scenarios in his mind. What if the man opened the door? What if she opened the door? What if they both opened the door? This last one he discounted. He knew there wasn't enough room for both to stand side by side. Still his mind whirred through the options.

He stopped and looked over the rail and down to the large lobby four levels below. Give them a minute or two to relax he thought, but not too long. He knew if he waited too long, one of the crew could spot him here, and his plans would have to change. That would not be a good thing.

"Time's up," he whispered and went to the door.

He knocked with his left hand and held the knife down by his side in his right hand. The woman opened the door, and as soon as it was about a third open, Ed attacked, crashing against the door and knocking the woman off balance. Without hesitation, he jumped forward jamming the end of the blade into the woman's flesh under the jaw. The blade didn't go deep; he didn't want to kill the woman now. He needed her alive to control the man.

She instinctively fought against him and reached for the knife, but as she did he slid behind her, jamming the blade of the knife a little further into her.

"Stop, or I'll kill you," Ed said, twisting the knife and feeling the woman's blood spill onto his hand.

The woman winced and went still. The door clicked shut behind them.

"Good, move over here," Ed pulled her over between the bed and the wall that separated the bathroom from the rest of the cabin. The narrow space didn't leave much room for maneuvering, but it also limited the attack options, if the woman's partner chose to sacrifice the woman to save himself. Ed quickly pulled the knife out from the flesh under the woman's jaw and pressed it against her throat. He pulled her back tight against him.

Chapter 38

When we entered the cabin, I went straight into the bathroom, started the shower, and began to undress. I couldn't shake the feeling that something was wrong and wondered why. I knew we should be safe in our room, and the killer should either be in custody by now or hiding somewhere. Still, the feeling wouldn't go away.

Over the noise of the shower, I thought I heard Rose say something. While waiting to see if she might say something more, I heard and felt something happening outside the bathroom door. For a second, I thought she may have fallen.

"Rose, what's up? Rose." I opened the bathroom door and looked out. The door to the cabin was closed. I stepped out and looked around the edge of the wall into the main part of the cabin. A chill rocketed through my body.

I saw Rose standing in the small space between the bed and the wall. A man held Rose from behind and had a knife pressed against her throat. Blood streamed down her neck and dripped from under her mouth onto the man's hand. I recognized the man immediately, and I had the impression he recognized me.

"Get over there," the man said, or something like that. My mind couldn't focus on what he said, but I understood him when he nodded his head toward the balcony.

"Wait a second, mister. You don't have to do this," I said and slowly walked to the balcony doors.

Rose must have sensed what the man had in mind and started squirming. The man reacted by pressing the knife against her throat so hard he cut deeper into her skin, and more blood spread down her throat.

"Don't do it!" I growled.

"Go out to the balcony," the man said.

For a split second, it seemed like time froze, and my mind raced to find my best options. Instead of coming up with a solution, I kept thinking of all the movie and television scenes where the bad guy had the woman hostage, similar to what was happening right now in front of me. The bad guy tells the good guy to drop his weapon, and ninety percent of the time in the movies, the good guy drops his weapon. All the while, I'm watching, shaking my head, and thinking, "What an idiot. Now he's going to kill them both. Just shoot the bad guy."

Now that good guy was me, but I didn't have a gun. I didn't have anything. Standing ten feet away from a killer in my underwear, I knew if I charged him, he wouldn't hesitate to kill her. I could probably take him, but she would be dead.

"Don't listen to him, Jim," Rose said. Her voice sounded strained, and her eyes clearly expressed the fear she had for what she anticipated her assailant's next command would be.

I opened the door to the balcony and took a step out. "Let her go," I said.

"Over the balcony, or she dies here tonight," the killer said. His face showed no emotion, but I felt like he was enjoying this.

"Don't do it, Jim. He'll kill me later anyway. No reason for us both to die," Rose said.

"No, no, young lady, I have no reason to kill you. I want to get to know you," the killer said. "And you, Jim, or whatever your name is, you want to come for me right now, you're welcome to try. I'll slice her throat open, and then you and I can fight over the knife while she bleeds to death. You might win, you might not, but she will most certainly die. You want that, or do you want to take your chances in the sea? I'm sure there'll be another cruise ship going by tomorrow. Can you stay afloat for twenty-four hours?"

I looked at the man and once again weighed my options. The only chance Rose had was for me to go over the side. It would buy her time and possibilities. I knew the odds were against me, but I didn't intend to die either. I started to climb over the railing.

"You'll survive the fall," Ed said.

"This will give you a chance, Rose," I shouted. I hung there while the wind pushed me both toward the stern of the ship and back against the balcony. Panic tried to overwhelm me, and for a moment, I felt my muscles freeze. I closed my eyes and strained to regain control.

My plan was simple. I never intended to reach the water below. During my last moments on the balcony and while hanging from it, I forced myself to focus on what I had to do. In theory, my plan seemed simple, but I knew it would be difficult and would never work if I lost my focus. I also wasn't kidding myself, I may have goofed off on the gymnastics equipment while in college, but I never was a gymnast. At the moment when I let go of the top railing, I wished I had been.

A second before letting go of the railing, I gripped the small space between the balcony floor and the Plexiglas side panel with my free hand. In theory, I should have been able to hang there and swing my legs inside the railing on the balcony below. Not a trick I'd recommend the average tourist try, but it seemed like a plausible, spur of the moment plan.

Unfortunately, my body mass, most likely aided by that last

banana split, produced too much downward momentum for the tips of the fingers on my right hand to maintain their grip. My effort to hold on did slow my fall, but it didn't give me enough time to swing my legs inside the guard rail below. It barely gave me enough time to bend my upper body forward before I continued downward. I caught the railing to the balcony below in both hands, but my ribs still crashed against the top rail. I used every ounce of strength I could to keep myself from bouncing off and away from the balcony. In that brief second of uncertainty, I locked the top of the railing under my left armpit.

Groaning, I climbed over to the safety of the balcony. The sliding glass door slid open, and a heavy set, bald man wearing pajamas stared at me with big eyes.

"How the hell did you get here?" he asked. "Are you okay?"

I stood up, but had to hold onto a deck chair to maintain my balance. I felt lightheaded, but after a few deep breaths I was able to speak. "Let me through, I need to get back to my cabin before he kills Rose. Call ship security."

He may have thought I was nuts, but he stepped away from the door and let me into his cabin.

"Who is he?" a woman in bed asked. She studied me like she didn't want to miss a detail when telling her friends about some crazy guy who landed on their cabin balcony.

I realized the man had gotten up from his bed to see what had happened. Both individuals were likely in their seventies and seemed more amazed at my arrival than concerned for their safety. I repeated my request for the man to call ship's security and to explain to them that the killer was in my cabin. I had him repeat the cabin number to me.

As I ran to the door to leave his cabin, I heard the woman ask her husband, "Why is he in his underwear?" I didn't wait to hear the answer.

Once in the hall, I sprinted to the stairs next to the elevators and raced up one deck. I didn't stop running until I slammed my shoulder into my cabin door in an attempt to break through. Despite the loud bang and shudder, the door held. I stepped back and kicked the door. I rushed both efforts and did little more than hurt my shoulder and foot.

I took a deep breath, trying to find the best place for my next kick, when two crewmen came running.

"What is going on?" the first to arrive asked.

"The man responsible for the murders on this ship is inside. He has Rose and is going to kill her." I started to kick the door, but the crewman grabbed my arm and motioned for his companion to unlock the door.

He stepped up with a master key card, but the door suddenly opened.

Chapter 39

Rose opened the door and looked out at us. The three of us stared back at her. The crewman closest to me actually took a step backward. Blood dripped from Rose's throat and covered almost all of her right arm. Blood had run down her blouse and splattered elsewhere onto her clothing. A small smear covered the left side of her face between her eye and her ear. I looked into her eyes, and her lips formed into a slight smile before she collapsed.

More people arrived behind us, and I heard loud talking. I ignored them and squatted next to Rose. She sat on the floor and leaned against the wall.

"I thought I lost you," she said softly.

"I'm okay. You hang in there," I squeezed her blood-soaked hand.

"Get a doctor," I ordered the group behind me, before I headed into the cabin in search of the killer. My first thought was that the coward must have jumped overboard rather than be captured. I imagined when he heard me slam into the door, he knew it was over. He must have stabbed Rose and then jumped overboard to escape capture.

The slight possibility that he may yet survive and escape infuriated me. The thought came to me that he may have tried to do what I did, and I hurried toward the balcony. At the sliding glass door, I stopped in my tracks. He lay there on the floor between the bed and the window. He wasn't going anywhere.

I looked at Rose. A crewman was helping her to her feet and

led her out of the room. The crowd at the door moved aside and let them out. Once she was through the doorway, Jerry Bergren entered the room with two of his security team.

"Stay here and don't let anyone in," he said to the two men. "What happened?" he asked me.

I didn't answer right away, and Jerry didn't say anything after he saw the body.

"She didn't have a choice," I said, breaking the silence.

"Rose did this?"

"Yes. The last I saw that guy had a knife to her throat and threatened to kill her, if I didn't go over."

He looked at me like he didn't understand, and I nodded at the balcony. He looked through the sliding glass door. "In your underwear?"

"Yes. I didn't have a choice. He had already cut her neck, and she was bleeding a lot. He told me to jump, or he would kill her."

"If he's our killer, he wouldn't have hesitated to kill her. What choice did you have?"

"Bergren!" A man at the door shouted. "Tell your men to let us in."

"It's okay, let them in," Jerry said to his men at the door. Turning back to me, he whispered, "our visiting, home office experts."

We both backed away from the body. "It's all yours, Sinclair."

Jerry put his arm on the back of my shoulder, "Why don't you come with me."

I grabbed a cruise line issued, white robe and my sandals from the closet as we walked by and followed him out the door. A crowd of curious passengers had gathered outside the cabin, but they readily gave way to let us pass through. I didn't look at any of them and didn't answer the questions a few asked as we went by.

"Can we go see Rose first?" I asked.

"Yes."

My mind spun with a thousand questions. I knew I should have felt relief with the way everything had ended, but if anything, I felt disoriented. Once on the elevator, I noticed Bergren watching me closely.

"Are you going to be okay?"

"Just worried about Rose," I said, but I knew there was more than that going on.

"Do you know why Anderson went after you two?"

"No," I said without thinking. I would think later.

We went the rest of the way to the infirmary without conversation and were immediately led into a treatment room where a nurse treated the wounds on Rose's neck. Rose had her eyes shut, but I saw that she wasn't hooked up to any machines to monitor her.

The doctor stepped into the room. "She'll be okay. I gave her a pain killer that's keeping her a little drowsy, but her vitals were fine. Despite all the blood on her, her wounds are not life threatening, and she shouldn't need a transfusion. She's awake."

"His blood," I said.

The doctor hadn't been briefed on everything. "Will I have another patient?" he asked Bergren.

"Not one you need to worry about. He's dead. Just the throat and arms on her?

"Yes. Defensive wounds to the forearms, and some of them nasty slices but not too deep. There is a stab wound under the mouth," he said and touched a spot on his upper throat. "It's the worst of the lot and could've done a lot of damage if the blade, a knife, right?" The doctor paused for an answer, and we both nodded. "If it had been pushed in deeper."

"He needed to keep her alive long enough to get rid of me," I said.

I could tell the doctor wanted to ask me something, but Bergren spoke first. "Doc, check him out real quick, will you?"

"I'm fine," I said.

"Won't take a second," the doctor said and led me over to a chair. "Take off the robe and let me take a look at you."

I removed my robe and hung it over the back of the chair. Glancing up, I saw Rose looking at me. She smiled but didn't say anything. The nurse, who had stopped working for a second, gently positioned Rose's head back to where she was looking straight up.

"A second visit," the doctor said. "We don't get too many repeat visitors. How's your face doing?" He glanced at my face and touched his earlier work.

"It's fine."

He stepped back and studied me. "I can see your problem already."

"What?" I said, glancing down at my chest and stomach. I could see the new bruising across the middle of my torso. "You're not going to tell me I need to lose weight are you?"

"That, too, but I think you have bruised some ribs, or possibly worse." He reached out, grabbing the blood pressure machine and rolled it over next to us. Before he hooked it up on me, he went through the routine of listening to my heart, my breathing, and shined a light into my eyes. As he wrapped the blood pressure straps around my arm, he asked, "How did you bruise your ribs?"

I told him, and he smiled as if my answer explained more about my condition. He pushed on a couple spots where the bruising had become more pronounced. I was sore around my bruising, but the pain wasn't significant.

"Wait here for a minute," he said and left the room. I looked back at Rose and watched the nurse apply stitches under her chin. Bergren had left, but one of his men stood by the door. I wondered if that was to keep us in or to protect us from others.

"Here you go," the doctor said when he reentered the room. He handed me a small glass.

I sniffed the contents. "Cognac?" I asked, and he smiled.

"Better for you right now than some pill. You've had an experience that put your adrenalin into hyper drive. Your injuries seem to be mild, unless you've got some other injury you haven't told me about."

I shook my head.

"You're coming down from an extreme adrenalin high. I'm surprised your hands aren't shaking more than they are."

I looked at my hands and saw that they were shaking. "I've been a little dizzy, too."

"All to be expected. You know, we frown on our passengers climbing around on the outside of our balconies. By the way, the cognac is a good Spanish one, and that's the only glass I'm giving you, so enjoy it." He raised his hand which held a glass and offered a toast. "Cheers." We clicked our glasses together.

The doctor inspected the work the nurse had done on Rose before he left the room. I sipped on the cognac and waited. The cognac felt warm going down, and I took some deep breaths in an attempt to further relax. I didn't know what was next and didn't care. At the moment, waiting to be alone with Rose became my sole objective.

"Are you going to be fine?"

I opened my eyes and looked up from the chair at the nurse. "Yes, I was trying to make sense of everything," I said.

"Good luck on that. This has been the craziest cruise I've ever been on. Did you say you dropped from one balcony to another?"

"It wasn't something I wanted to do."

"I hope that doesn't show up on Facebook, or we'll have dozens of stupid copycats trying it and getting killed," she said, shaking her head. "We're done. I'm going to recommend that she be allowed to go back to her cabin. Are you two together?" she asked.

"Yes, I'll get her back safely," I said and wondered how dumb that sounded. I hadn't done a very good job so far.

"Okay," she said and left, closing the door behind her.

I looked over at Rose, and she was looking at me.

"Don't ever do that again," she said, her voice sounded stronger than I expected.

"What?"

"I thought I lost you. I thought that you killed yourself in some stupid, stupid act of chivalry. Don't ever do that again."

"What was I supposed to do? He would have killed you. I really believe he would not have hesitated to kill you."

"I don't care," she said.

"What would you have done if the roles were reversed?"

"That's not what we're talking about. I don't want to have anyone sacrifice themselves for me. I don't want to have to live with that. If one of us gets to live, then that's not me. Understand?"

She looked a hundred percent serious, and I thought the conversation was a stupid one. Of course I would do it again, and I believe if the roles were reversed, she would have done what I did.

"It it makes any difference, I never planned on jumping into the ocean. I thought I would just climb down to the balcony below. I had to do something to give you a chance. I returned with reinforcements, but you didn't need saving."

"He killed the missing woman, too."

"What?" The topic changed too quickly for me. "He admitted to killing the woman?"

"Unless there is someone else missing or dead."

"What did he say?"

"He said, four down, that's got to be a record. His exact words."

"The crewman, Joe, the woman, and me, that's four alright," I said. "You would have been five."

"He wanted to rape me first, the stupid idiot. That was his mistake," Rose said. "As soon as you disappeared, he pushed me down toward the bed. A big mistake because he removed the knife from my throat as he did." She stopped talking, but I could see that she took advantage of whatever separation she had to go on the offensive.

"I just want us to go back to our cabin and go to sleep," I said.

"You know that's not going to happen."

For a second, I worried if she was mad at me, but then the obvious became clear. We would be spending the next couple of hours being interviewed and re-interviewed.

"Are you going to be okay enough to go through a lengthy interview tonight?" I asked.

"Yes," she lifted her arms and looked at the half dozen bandages that covered both arms. "The only bad one was here." She touched the spot under her jaw. "He was quick, quicker than I would've expected for a man his age."

The door opened and three men in cruise ship uniforms entered. I didn't recognize any of them. The nurse who had treated Rose followed them into the room.

"Mr. West, I need you to come with me," one of the men said.

Chapter 40

My interview lasted an hour, and they had me wait for another forty five minutes before letting me leave. Since I felt somewhat reassured that Rose was going to be okay, I had plenty of time to become self-conscious about still only wearing my underwear under an ill-fitting bathrobe.

"I imagine we'll need a different cabin tonight," I said, before walking out of the interview room.

The security guy they sent back to let me go, one I finally recognized, Henri from the first of my many meetings with Jerry's staff, looked confused for a second.

"Oh, sorry," he said. "They've kind of cut us out of things now. Fresh eyes and ears they claim, but I think that since it's now looking like we can wrap it up, they want to be there as a big part of the solution." He rolled his eyes. "Follow me."

We turned down a hall and went into a room on the right. Inga sat behind a desk typing into a computer. She looked up at me and smiled.

"What's this I hear about you letting Rose do all the hard work?"

"I've always wanted to see the ship from the outside, and it seemed like a good time to jump from balcony to balcony." I tried to grin, but my heart wasn't into it. "No, actually it's all quite complicated."

"I got him from here," she said to Henri, and he left. She studied me for a second. "I'm sorry to make light of it. I shouldn't have, but I had the advantage of hearing about it after it was all over, and you two were okay. It must have been terrifying. I'm sorry."

"No need to be sorry," I said. "The quicker we can get over the experience the better it will be for us, too."

"What can I do for you, Jim?"

I explained our predicament with the room being a crime scene and needing a place to spend the night. She picked up the phone on her desk and called whoever was in charge of the cabins on the ship but didn't like the answer she was given.

"Would you mind waiting here for a minute? I want to see if I can fix this," she said.

"I have nowhere to go. Could you also try to find out where Rose is at the moment?"

She said she would and left the room. Five minutes later, she returned. "Want to hear the good news or the bad news?"

"The good news, please," I said, having little patience for games.

"Rose will be here in a minute or two. They've finished talking to her, and the nurse is taking one last look at her before she gets the okay to go. The nurse will bring her here."

I didn't plan on asking her for the bad news, and Bergren's entrance into the office changed our conversation. "How are you feeling?" he asked.

"I'm okay," I said. "Just need to take a shower and get to bed."

He nodded. "I'm worried about Rose," he said. "Did you get a good look at the deceased?"

"I couldn't see much," I said. I could have added that at the time all I could think of was how satisfying it felt that the guy was dead.

"She didn't just stab him. She stabbed him nearly a dozen

times," he said. "This may be hard for her to get over. I think it would be good for her to get some counseling for a while."

"I think the last eight or nine stabbings was the therapy she needed, but I understand what you're saying. I'll recommend counseling."

"Good. I'm also concerned the interview may have been a little rough on her. They took it out of our hands," he said.

"Is she good to go, though? You can't be holding her," I said.

"You're both good to go. I wouldn't have stood for her being held for anything, but there may be more questions."

"There always are."

"I'll see you in the morning, Jim," he said and left.

"When Rose gets here, I'll take you back to your cabin so you can get whatever you need, and then I'll take you to the cabin we have for you tonight. It's not a great one, sorry," Inga said.

"If that was the bad news, don't worry about it. I just need clean sheets and a comfortable bed. I'm sure that the room will be fine with Rose, too."

"I imagine this wasn't the cruise you had in mind when you booked it," she said, trying to make small talk while we waited.

"That probably goes for you, too. Any new word on the fallout from all this?"

"I'm too far down in the chain to know exactly, but I'm being transferred to a different ship. I'm being told it's not a punishment, but I don't know."

"You'll be fine," I said. "No way they can blame any of this on you."

"That's what Jerry says, but still," she didn't finish her statement.

"At least everything is wrapped up. All they have to do now

is the paperwork, and of course, finish all the second guessing."

"How about the missing woman?" Inga asked.

"This guy Anderson did that, too. He bragged to Rose that I was his fourth, that he thought it was some kind of record. I guess he meant no one else had ever committed four murders on a cruise before. Rose would have been number five."

"He was a monster. I would've stabbed him a dozen times, too."

Rose arrived a few minutes later, looking exhausted and not in the best of moods. I stood up to go, but Rose plopped down on a chair.

"Whenever you're ready, Inga will take us to get what we need from our room tonight and then on to a new room," I said.

Rose looked at me with a tired smile. "Will you go and find me a coke, please. I need some sugar just to give me enough energy to go to sleep."

"Sure," I said and left the room. Rose did look like a coke could help, but I also felt she wanted a few minutes to talk to Inga.

I remembered seeing an outdoor soda dispenser near one of the dining areas. When I returned, nobody at the reception area or in the first couple of offices stopped me or asked me what I was doing. I guess I had been there so many times they all considered me part of the team.

I knocked on the door and heard Inga say to come in.

As I entered, both women stood up, and Inga walked around her desk and gave Rose a hug. I gave Rose her coke, and Ingrid led us out of her office.

"Sorry, Jim, I needed to vent, and I did want a coke," Rose said.

"You know you can always vent to me, too."

"I know, but I needed a woman's reassurance in this case."

"Still mad at me?" I asked.

"Not so much," she said. "Not anymore."

Chapter 41

The small, interior cabin had no windows. When we got into bed and turned off the lights, we couldn't see anything.

"This may sound silly, but do you want me to turn on the bathroom light so it won't be so dark in here?"

"No, this is fine," Rose said. She rolled over and snuggled up to me. "I just want to sleep tonight, Jim."

"Okay," I said.

"I don't know why I stabbed him so many times. That's what everyone kept asking me."

"Better to be safe than sorry," I said.

"He pushed me back onto the bed and reached for my blouse. I knew what he planned to do before he killed me. I just reacted. He never expected that, I suppose."

"His mistake."

"You know what's interesting? I never thought I would use all that training. You know, I took most of those self-defense classes because the guys did. I wanted to be as tough as the male deputies."

"You are, and there's nothing wrong with that."

"The guy was sick, Jim. He got aroused when he was standing behind me holding a knife to my throat, and you were going overboard. At the time, I wondered if killing you was what got him excited." She paused for a second, but I didn't interrupt. "I bit him, too. When I grabbed his knife hand, and we struggled for a second, he fell on top of me on the bed. I bit the side of his neck.

I bit it hard, and that's when he let go of the knife to push away."

"Biting is fair in situations like that."

"I got the knife and started stabbing him. We rolled off the other side of the bed, and I kept stabbing him. I just kept stabbing him."

I kissed her forehead. A minute later, I could hear the deep breathing and knew that somehow she had fallen asleep.

I woke at seven, my internal alarm clock still as frustratingly accurate as usual. Rose still slept, and I managed to get out of bed without disturbing her. In the dark room, I carefully worked my way around to the bathroom, realizing as I did that the ship had stopped moving.

When I finished in the bathroom, I left the light on, so I could see to get dressed. Picking up my cell phone, I noticed a message from Sarah. The text simply read, "Can I see you this morning?" It also included a photo of a man in his underpants trying to kick in a door.

"You got to be kidding," I said out loud.

"What?" Rose asked.

"Sorry, I didn't mean to wake you."

"I was awake. What's up?"

I showed Rose my phone, and she grinned. "Trying to rescue me in your underpants? How sweet. Hope they're clean, because you know people can zoom in."

"I hope that doesn't get blasted everywhere around on the internet."

"Too late for that I'm sure. Where else would Sarah have gotten it? It'll probably be on TV tonight."

I groaned, and someone knocked on the door.

"Kind of early for visitors," Rose said.

I opened the door and was greeted by a member of the crew whom I recognized from my many trips by the reception desk.

"Good morning," she said. "Captain Niemann invites you and Ms. Luna to join him for breakfast in his private dining room at seven thirty. He said to tell you it's important."

"Tell him we'll be there," Rose shouted from the bed.

I didn't need to as our guest heard her. "I'll be back at seven twenty five to guide you there. Would that be alright?"

We both smiled and waited for Rose to answer. "Okay, thank you," Rose said.

The receptionist winked at me before she turned and left. I nodded at the crewman sitting guard outside our door.

"You know we have a guard outside the door just like Sarah has," I said to Rose, while she got out of bed.

"To protect us, or so we can't get away?"

"Let's hope he's there so no one disturbs us and nothing more serious," I said. "You know, I left my razor in our cabin." I rubbed my chin, looking at my face in the mirror.

"You're on a ship. Beards are acceptable. Look at me, I need a turtle neck sweater or a large scarf to cover my throat and these bandages," Rose said and pushed by me to get to the bathroom.

"I've always liked choke collars."

The look she gave me, as she disappeared into the bathroom, indicated that my comment hadn't impressed her. "Juvenile," she said loud enough for me to hear after the door closed.

We weren't alone with Captain Niemann during breakfast. Sarah was already there having coffee with him when we arrived. The entire breakfast experience was first class, the room, the fine china, and even a server standing nearby to pour more coffee or bring an extra piece of toast.

The conversation began with the captain apologizing to Sarah and then to Rose. Rose shifted the conversation to the small, private dining room we were in, and for the rest of the meal, we talked about the various dining rooms and difficulties of feeding thousands of people every day. At one point, the captain had his chef come in and answer questions concerning the preparation of food on the ship. Finally as if on cue, Johann Needles arrived to escort Rose away, and a little later, Barbara Brian showed up for Sarah.

"Am I on my own?" I asked

"Not necessarily, another cup of coffee and a donut? I'll be having one," Captain Niemann offered.

I never figured out whether he was keeping me there for any special reason, or if he really just wanted company before he had to face the world, too. Either way, I enjoyed the extra half hour. He did explain that Sarah had to deal with a mountain of paperwork that his staff and some officials from Galveston would help her get through. Rose, too, would be tied up for some time with both local and federal authorities, and that his staff would assist her in any way they could.

Everyone involved, other than Sarah and Rose, had expressed the desire to keep me away, or as Captain Niemann put it, "They didn't think you needed to be involved."

A small part of me wanted to protest and say I was an important piece of everything, but common sense won out. I realized sitting there with the captain and eating a donut was a much better way to pass the time.

Before I left him, I had one question. "So, what are your plans now?"

"It's been suggested I take some of my built up vacation days.

I plan to do so, and given a little time, I think there's a good chance that I'll end up with another ship. With the investigation now resolved, I'm hoping the aftertaste from this tragedy won't linger all that long."

"I hope it doesn't either. None of this was anyone's fault but Anderson's." I was preaching to the choir, so I shut up, thanked him, and wandered back to our cabin, hoping they no longer considered it a crime scene.

A man I didn't recognize, wearing civilian attire, stood guard just outside the cabin door. I didn't see any tape across the open doorway, although I did hear the sound of a vacuum or steam cleaner coming from inside the room.

"Mr. West?" the man asked, and after I said I was, he introduced himself. "I'm Detective Bob Hicks with the Galveston city police. Everyone just left, so I think you're free to go in and get your stuff."

"What are you still doing here?"

"Bureaucracy, you know, and some bullshit," he said with a grin. "I'm just waiting for someone to tell me I can leave. My guess is that will happen shortly after this morning's press conference, and more importantly, after the Chief has said that the department still has someone here working the crime scene."

"Seems to be a quick turnaround on the crime scene."

"It all happened outside US jurisdiction, and the cruise line believes everything has been resolved," Hicks said.

"I guess that makes sense. Want a chair?" I asked.

"Sure," he said, and I went into the room and brought out two chairs.

"You waiting for your lady friend, the deputy?"

"Yep," I said.

"Must be one tough lady. I understand she kicked the guy's butt, and he had a knife to her. He'd already cut her up some, too, is that right?"

"Yep," I said, getting pretty relaxed with this conversation.

"He'd already killed, what did they say three, four people?"

"Three. I was supposed to be four and Rose five."

He looked at me for a minute. "Damn, that's right. You climbed down the side of the ship while it was still out at sea. Man, I couldn't have done that. That took guts, but you got to give it to, what's the deputy's name, Rose?"

"That's it."

"You got to give it to her, killed that guy with his own knife. You two married?"

"No."

"I don't know, but she sounds like a keeper to me," he said.

"Yeah, she is. She really is."

"You said you're waiting for her?"

I nodded. "For as long as it takes."

"Hope you don't mind, but I want to meet this lady friend of yours."

"Don't mind, don't mind at all."

"Do they have room service here?" he asked. "I missed breakfast this morning."

"What do you want?" I said, grinning.

Title: *Dead Men Can Kill*™
- Author: Bob Doerr
- Publisher: TotalRecall Publications, Inc.
- Paper Back: ISBN: 978-1-59095-759-2
- Book: ISBN: 978-1-59095-761-5
- Number of pages: 320
- Publication: December 8, 2009

When Jim West, a former Air Force Special Agent with the Office of Special Investigations, moves back to New Mexico, his goal is simple: start an easy going second career as a professional lecturer on investigative techniques to colleges and civic organizations. He never envisioned that his practical demonstration of forensic hypnosis on stage with a state university student would stir up memories of an 18-year old murder mystery. When the student is murdered three days later, West finds himself ensnared in a web of intrigue that pits him and the small town's authorities against a ruthless, psychotic killer.

An aggressive reporter for the town newspaper seeks out West for help with the story, but after one of her co-workers is murdered, she quickly aligns her efforts with West and the Sheriff. As West works closely with her, he begins to wonder if this could be the first real relationship for him since his devastating divorce a few years earlier.

The killer, though, has other plans for the reporter and the story takes fascinating twists and turns, leading to an inevitable, riveting confrontation.

Look out for a new hero on the mystery/thriller landscape! Jim West, retired military investigator, is resourceful, intuitive, pragmatic and always competent. All of West's abilities are tested when he matches wits with psychopathic serial killer William White, a man whose appreciation for murder is surpassed only by his delight in domination. Bob Doerr has crafted a must-read addition to the genre in Dead Men Can Kill, which evolves from absorbing story to absolute page-turner as West closes in on a killer who is supposedly dead. Highly recommended!

--Dallin Malmgren, author of...
The Whole Nine Yards   The Ninth Issue   Is This for a Grade?

A Jim West™ Mystery/Thriller

Title: *Cold Winter's Kill*™
- Author: Bob Doerr
- Publisher: TotalRecall Publications, Inc.
- Paper Back: ISBN: 978-1-59095-763-9
- Book: ISBN: 978-1-59095-764-6
- Number of pages: 288
- Publication: Dec 8, 2009

Cold Winter's Kill is a fast-paced thriller that takes place in the scenic mountains of Lincoln County, New Mexico and throws Jim West into a race against time to stop a psychopath who abducts and kills a young blonde every Christmas...

It was one of those phone calls former Air Force Special Agent Jim West never wanted to receive--an old friend calling to ask if he could drive down to Ruidoso, New Mexico to help locate his daughter who has disappeared while on a ski trip with friends. Jim found himself heading to Ruidoso even though he believed, much like the local authorities, that if she had gone missing in the mountains in December, her survival chances were slim. He didn't want to be there when they found her, but still he drove on.

Once in Ruidoso, Jim discovers a sinister coincidence that changes everything. It appears that someone is abducting and killing one young blond every year around Christmas. The race is on--can Jim locate his friend's daughter in time? But why is this happening and who's doing it?

Jim can't wait for the local authorities to raise the priority of their search, or for the pending blizzard to pass. In his haste he puts himself in the killer's sights. Will he, too, suffer from a cold winter's kill?

"GREAT SUSPENSE! In *Cold Winter's Kill* Bob Doerr grabs your attention from the beginning and holds it until the last sentence. Hard to put down!"

> *--Shelba Nicholson*
> former Women's Editor, *Texarkana Gazette*

A Jim West™ Mystery/Thriller

Title: *Loose Ends Kill*™

- Author: Bob Doerr
- Publisher: TotalRecall Publications, Inc.
- Paper Back: ISBN: 978-1-59095-718-9
- Book: ISBN: 978-1-59095-719-6
- Number of pages: 288
- Publication: Oct 27, 2010

LOOSE ENDS KILL **is a fast-paced mystery/thriller** that takes place in the historic city of San Antonio, Texas, and throws Jim West into the middle of a police investigation of the murder of an old friend's wife. The police already believe they have the killer in custody – West's friend.

West is drawn into this mystery by a call from the old friend who requests his assistance. West agrees to help his friend and digs deep to try to find another suspect. In the process he soon discovers that he is being followed and targeted for harassment, but by whom?

West quickly discovers that he didn't know his old friend's wife as well as he thought. To his surprise, he learns that she has had a number of affairs dating back for more than a decade. In fact, while investigating the murder, he realizes that his friend and he may be the only two people unaware of her philandering behavior.

Theorizing that one of her lovers could have had just as much motive as her husband, West starts turning over the rocks identifying one lover after another. In doing so, West unintentionally ignites an outbreak of more death and mayhem. The police and his friend's lawyers want West to go back home. The police even threaten to arrest him.

Soon, West believes the real killer wants him gone or dead. Deciding the only way to resolve the case before the outside pressures force him to leave, he sets a trap for the killer using himself as bait. However, he soon learns he may have only outsmarted himself.

A Jim West™ Mystery/Thriller

Title: *Another Colorado Kill*™

- Author: Bob Doerr
- Publisher: TotalRecall Publications, Inc.
- Paper Back: ISBN: 978-1-59095-785-1
- Book: ISBN: 978-1-59095-786-8
- Number of pages: 288
- Publication Date: September 06, 2011

It was supposed to be a short, fun golf outing, but when Jim West and his friend Edward "Perry" Mason stumble across a dead body in a restroom at a rest stop along I-25, things turn bad and then only get worse.

With the golf outing shot, West intends to stay in Colorado Springs only for a day or two. However, when two more murder victims turn up – one with West's name handwritten in her notebook - the heat on West skyrockets. The police instruct him to stick around, and soon he discovers that while the police may want to pin the crimes on him, the killer wants him out of the picture. Way out – like dead.

West's only ally is Lieutenant Michelle Prado, a tall red head with large green eyes that captivate West. Assigned to keep an eye on West, Lieutenant Prado decides the best way to do so is to keep him close. West and Prado do their own digging into the investigation. In the process, Jim wonders how close their relationship will evolve.

It seems to West that as the police focus less on him, the killer intensifies his focus on him. Barely surviving an initial confrontation, West realizes he must take the initiative. If he doesn't, or perhaps even if he does - he may end up as just another Colorado kill.

A Jim West™ Mystery/Thriller

Title: *No One Else To Kill*™
- Author: Bob Doerr
- Publisher: TotalRecall Publications, Inc.
- Paper Back: ISBN: 978-1-59095-423-2
- eBook: ISBN: 978-1-59095-424-9
- Number of pages in the finished book: 352
- Publication Date: December 4, 2012

No One Else to Kill, **Bob Publications** - In this newest West series, Mr. West finds out of town. Looking forward to reservation at the remote in the Pecos Wilderness area in hunter's haven. Expecting to do relax, he has no idea what the holds for him. When a murder guest are detained and no one is sheriff is called in, and while the

Doerr, TotalRecall book in the popular Jim himself stood up and some R & R he keeps his hunting lodge. Located New Mexico it's a nothing other than rest of the weekend takes place, the hotel beyond suspicion. The investigation is

underway, a second murder takes place. Both crimes are clearly related, but by whom and why? With time running out and unable to find a motive, the legal experts seek Jim's help.

The cover for *No One Else To Kill* is a 2013 finalist for the da Vinci Eye award.

Bob's four previous novels in the series are titled *Dead Men Can Kill, Cold Winter's Kill, Loose Ends Kill,* and *Another Colorado Kill.* The latter two were selected as Eric Hoffer Award finalists for 2010 and 2011, respectively.

Bob Doerr's *No One Else To Kill* was awarded the Grand Prize in the "Books With Out Publishers" writing contest at www.ultimateherocontest.com

A Jim West™ Mystery/Thriller

Title: *Caffeine Can Kill*™
- Author: Bob Doerr
- Publisher: TotalRecall Publications, Inc.
- Paper Back: ISBN: 978-1-59095-562-8
- eBook: ISBN: 978-1-59095-563-5
- Number of pages in the finished book: 240
- Publication Date: 2017

This Jim West mystery/thriller, the sixth in the series, finds Jim traveling to the Texas Hill Country to attend the grand opening of a friend's winery and vineyard. Upon arriving in Fredericksburg, Jim witnesses a brutal kidnapping at a local coffee shop. The next morning while driving down an unpaved country road to the grand opening, he comes across an active crime scene barely a quarter mile from his friend's winery. A Fredericksburg policeman who talked to Jim the day before at the kidnapping scene recognizes Jim and asks him to identify the body of a dead young woman as the woman who was kidnapped. Jim does, and as a result of this unwelcome relationship with the police is asked the next morning to identify the body of another murdered person as the man who had kidnapped the young woman. A third murder throws Jim's vacation into complete disarray and draws Jim and a female friend into the sights of one of the killers.

A Jim West™ Mystery/Thriller

Title: *Greed Can Kill*™
- Author: Bob Doerr
- Publisher: TotalRecall Publications, Inc.
- Paper Back: ISBN: 978-1-59095-731-8
- eBook: ISBN: 978-1-59095-741-7
- Number of pages in the finished book: 280
- Publication Date: 2017

This adventure finds Jim traveling to Fabens, TX, in an effort to locate an old acquaintance who had written Jim a cryptic letter asking for his help in finding a briefcase. In Fabens, he discovers that someone has murdered his friend. Jim provides a copy of the letter to the local police explaining that he has no idea where the briefcase is or how to decipher the sets of numbers provided in the letter. Figuring there is nothing more he can do, Jim starts his trek back home. He plans to spend a night or two relaxing at the Lodge in Cloudcroft, NM, on his way only to find that he is being followed. An ominous, unidentified phone caller gives Jim an ultimatum - find the briefcase and turn it over to him within a week.

A violent confrontation in Cloudcroft verifies Jim's worst suspicion, a Mexican drug cartel wants the briefcase. The confrontation also brings the FBI into the picture. They also want Jim to continue his search. The search takes Jim to the New Mexican ghost town of Chloride where the final confrontation takes place and Jim finds out who the bad guys really are.

Author Bob Doerr Uses his special knowledge to provide authentic details in his novels about how law enforcement agencies do their work.

www.bobdoerr.com

A Jim West™ Mystery/Thriller

Title: *The Attack*™

- Author: Bob Doerr
- Publisher: TotalRecall Publications, Inc.
- Paper Back: ISBN: 978-1-59095-146-0
- Book: ISBN: 978-1-59095-147-7
- Number of pages in the finished book:
- Publication Date:

A terrorist team has just set off four explosive devices in an international airport close to New York City. The leader of the terrorists, Ahmad Khalin, survives the attack and plans to attack a second U.S. airport within the month. As Khalin makes his escape from the New York area he is involved in a shooting in Connecticut. Clint Smith, a U.S. government agent assigned to an ultra-secret agency, is at a restaurant across the street when the shooting occurs. He responds to the scene to see if he can help, but Khalin is gone. On a hunch, Teresa Deer, Smith's boss, sends Smith after Khalin. Smith's pursuit takes him to Bar Harbor, Maine; Wiesbaden, Germany; the Costa Brava, Spain; Northern Scotland; Lake of the Woods, Ontario, Canada; and finally into Saskatchewan, Canada, where the final confrontation takes place. Throughout the pursuit, a number of interesting characters add to the subplots and try to survive their involvement in the chase.

A Clint Smith Thriller™

Title: *The Group*™

- Author: Bob Doerr
- Publisher: TotalRecall Publications, Inc.
- Paper Back: ISBN: 978-1-59095-569-7
- eBook: ISBN: 978-1-59095-570-3
- Number of pages in the finished book: 288
- Publication Date: 2016

A fast-moving international thriller that pits a lone government operative, known as a hunter, against an unknown group of assassins who pose a worldwide threat.

Someone is killing off the world's rich and famous. The murders are sophisticated, requiring precision and skill. The international community is in an uproar but has no leads in its attempt to find the assassins. The victims were members of the Bilderberg Group, an international, loose knit group of the uber rich that meet annually. While the attacks have not had a direct impact on the U.S., Theresa Deer, Director of the Special Section, a small unit whose existence is known by only a handful in the U.S. government, sees this new age League of Assassins as a national threat. She sends her hunters out. Clint Smith finds their trail Switzerland where his discovery almost leads to his own death. The hunt leads him to Mallorca, Spain, where he witnesses a helicopter attack on a villa where a number of attendees from the Bilderberg conference were holding a follow-on meeting of their own. Smith picks up the trail a couple weeks later in Las Vegas, NV, and in his hunt finds out that he is no longer the hunter. He has become the prey.

A Clint Smith Thriller™

Title: *The assassins*™

- Author: Bob Doerr
- Publisher: TotalRecall Publications, Inc.
- Paper Back: ISBN: 9781590951965
- eBook: ISBN: 9781590951972
- Number of pages in the finished book: 242
- Publication Date: 2018

A disputed election has divided the nation, and a handful of senior government officials have conspired to have the North Koreans assassinate the President of the United States. Believing the assassination attempt to be only days away, Theresa Deer, Director of the Special Section, a small unit whose existence is known by only a few in the U.S. government, is tasked to interdict the man intent on providing the North Koreans vital information about the president's itinerary for his visit to South Korea. While Deer succeeds in her mission, she is severely injured and finds herself being hunted by the North Korean assassins. Clint Smith is sent to Korea to help Deer get back to the U.S. and finds himself caught in a deadly game of cat and mouse with the North Koreans. With no one in the U.S. government to turn to for help, and the South Koreans now also hunting them, getting out of South Korea alive is looking unlikely.

A Clint Smith Thriller™

Title: *The Enchanted Coin*™

- Author: Bob Doerr
- Publisher: TotalRecall Publications, Inc.
- Paper Back: ISBN: 978-1-59095-084-5
- Book: ISBN: 978-1-59095-085-2
- Audio Book Available:
- Number of pages in the finished book: 130
- Publication Date: September 17, 2013

We have all heard of tales of UFO's, ghosts, people who say they can talk to the spirits, ancient curses, and magical talismans. Most of us automatically dismiss them as false, figments of people's imagination, and understandably so. However, might not just a few of them be true? I don't know, but I heard this story from a young man the other day who swore the fascinating tale I have set forth in this book really did really occur, because it happened to him. You be the judge.

Title: *The Rescue of Vincent*™

- Author: Bob Doerr
- Publisher: TotalRecall Publications, Inc.
- Paperback, 6" x 9" ISBN: 978-1-59095-279-5
- eBook: ISBN: 978-1-59095-280-1
- Audio Book Available:
- Number of pages in the finished book: 160
- Publication Date: October 28, 2014

The Rescue of Vincent: Book 2 in The Enchanted Coin Series is a 31,000 word fantasy adventure targeted at Middle Grade readers. Imagine being a fourteen year old again and finding a coin that seems to give off a light of its own. The coin has your name on it, and instructs you to toss it into a fountain next to the Tree of Life. That's what happens in The Rescue of Vincent, and what starts my protagonist off on a magical adventure that many young boys and girls would love to have. This book is "G" rated.

Title: *The Magic of Vex*™

- Author: Bob Doerr
- Publisher: TotalRecall Publications, Inc.
- Paper Back: ISBN: 978-1-59095-309-9
- eBook: ISBN: 978-1-59095-280-1
- Audio ISBN: 978-1-59095-281-8
- Number of pages in the finished book: 140
- Publication Date: August 4, 2015

Samantha Gillespie's discovery of a magic coin results in her transportation to the strange world of Vex where magic is real and where she has to over-come a number of challenges if she ever hopes to return home.

What happened to Samantha was totally unexpected and quite frightening. It led her to an adventure that many might think impossible to believe, but it did.

You be the judge.

Locate Bob on Facebook and
let him know how you like his books.

Author Bob Doerr Uses his special knowledge to provide authentic
details in his novels about how law enforcement agencies do their
work.
For a complete list of books by Bob Doerr,
a preview of upcoming titles and more
visit his website.
www.bobdoerr.com

Titles by Bob Doerr

Mystery Detective Suspense Thrillers

Dead Men Can Kill
Cold Winters Kill
Another Colorado Kill
Loose Ends Kill
No One Else To Kill
Caffeine Can Kill
Greed Can Kill

Action Adventure Series

The Attack
The Group
The Assassins

Mouse Gate Series

The Enchanted Coin
The Rescue of Vincent
The Magic of Vex